GROUNDSCRATCHERS

STORIES BY
GABRIEL WELSCH

Tolsun Books
Flagstaff, Arizona

For David J. and Camille B. Welsch

TABLE OF CONTENTS

GROUNDSCRATCHERS
AND OTHER STORIES

HAUNT

Even her birth began as a rumor, her mother having left the small town to stain another locale, and the name she carried at birth was an echo of a family past few knew. Her nickname through childhood, Gizzen, for her Cheshire grin, came from the marginal language spoken only in the alleys of her birth city. An old lover had hanging on his wall a framed document, large as a quarto page, on how to butcher a horse. The lines divided a ghost outline into chops and roasts and other equine delights. She was barely more than a girl when she asked him about it, and he let smoke curl up into his nose as he told her she would develop an appreciation for all the world has forgotten.

She later bought a pair of ancient shoes from a woman with a German accent at a yard sale, and tucked in the toe was a letter she eventually learned enough German to read. The letter mentioned casting dill and salt in the shoes as a charm against woe, and she read it to her husband the night before he left for war. She never used the language afterward, she learned to speak of

3

her husband in the past tense, and then not at all, and the shoes lost the scent of dill.

Returning to the street of her childhood, she discovered it to be an *alleé* of maples. The rows had to have been there when she was young, but they had never grown in the image she'd held in her mind and for years thought was true. When she lay on the last bed in which she'd ever sleep, sore because those who were supposed to move her came less and less to the dark shape of her room, she understood that to be alive—as a person, a language, a custom, a place—is to forget.

TWINS

1.

No one who lives here really notices the twins of Walkchalk unless someone new comes to town and asks about them. It goes the same way each time. The newcomer is standing in line waiting for a booth at Hartley's, or at the checkout at Toy's, or maybe driving out to the fire hall and sees them on one of their walks. Then the person turns, always that thoughtful look, that bunched up face, that look—even if that person has only been here for a little while, a weekend, a day, a few hours—the look that asks, *why didn't you say anything about this,* before pulling it together to ask, "What's the story with those two?"

Story. Well, people usually say, there's a lot of stories. They've been around forever. Some have heard that they were born here, orphaned, sisters raised by well-meaning but crazy spinsters who lived in a run-down farm and let the twins run through the woods. They're in their seventies now, hunched over, barely five feet tall. They mumble to one another in gibberish and a lot of clawing motions with their fingers and hand-waving and so on. We know enough from TV that they have some kind of twin language. Not that there has ever been a TV program on them. We just knew it from seeing other programs on strange but true things about twins. But the strange-but-true twins on those programs always live in cities.

No one would come here for TV. They came for a movie once a few years ago. A horror film based on a true story. They needed a town that looked like a West Virginia mining town from the late 1960s. They only had to change a few of the lights on our bridge, take down a few signs, and there it was. Right where we'd always been.

The twins always carry long paper bags, like extra tall grocery bags. Some say there are just clothes in them—but whatever they're carrying around, it can't weigh much of anything. They're too frail to be able to carry anything more than a few items. They once saw a pair of twin babies at the church's strawberry festival. They went over and starting muttering at the babies while the parents, pretty new to town, and from the city, tried to grin. Everybody could tell looking at them that they wanted it to be over and for the twins to be on their way. But then one of them tried to pick up a baby. She could barely lift it, and as the mother started to swoop in to grab the baby away, the twin dropped it. The child started wailing and people grumbled and the twins grabbed their bags and tottered off, grabbing a few plates of shortcake as they passed the serving table.

Everyone knew that story at one point. The same summer a girl disappeared from the folk festival and the twins started stealing girls' blouses and pants in clear daylight from the clotheslines

6

in Applewold. Everyone heard the story of how the twins loved babies, loved baby girls, would coo and sputter affection and spittle over babies when parents let them draw near enough.

It was the same year we built a fence in our yard. We told people it was for the dog, even though the dog by then was too old to walk much let alone run out into the road. No one knew we were expecting, that some biological door that had until then been closed had opened in one or the other of us, that we were to have a child, and then we soon knew it would be children, and then we soon after that knew it would be two girls, and that they would be our princesses.

2.

The twins walked everywhere, unable to drive, having undone the patience and charity of a string of careworkers, and having frustrated the efforts of different agencies to put them in group homes or other situations, they wound up with no means of transport, no money, and, it appeared, no concerns about either condition. They moved out of every halfway house or home into which they had been placed, sometimes forcibly. They lived in bathrooms. For a while, it was Walmart, where they would bathe out of sinks and sleep under the sinks. The employees didn't say anything, worked around them, had no idea, really, what to do about them. Then their district manager showed up ranting about "a public health menace" and how Walmart "is not a goddamned charity. We give to charity, we do not become one." After that, workers started leaving food out for them. The district manager, as far as anyone knows, is still not aware of the effect of his inspirational speech.

The women lived at Hartley's for a while, until another man-ager—this time the night manager—finally hustled them off because people waiting in line for a table could smell them. In the summer months, they take to the woods. Those who notice them at that time of the year point out the twig stuck in one's hair, or the grass stains on a lavender cardigan, things like that. People have found them in their barns, in detached garages, underneath decks, in hunting cabins—their resourcefulness is almost equal to that of a cat or a rodent. No one has ever heard of anyone getting really angry at them. Everyone knows what they're like, that they mean no harm, that people are probably safe around them. But they are no saints, either. Without fail, when someone discovers the twins, barns and sheds are locked, new doors are put on garages, hunting camps are boarded up more securely for the season, decks are fenced. There are no spectacular scenes of eviction, just the usual moderate cruel-ties, the passive rejection that looks to everyone, and what we know too well people tell themselves—just looking out for ev-eryone concerned. It's not safe.

Our own girls have started to walk, to ramble and troll the backyard, to turn over leaves and find slugs, to chase the purple balls that almost float in the grass. They are princesses, fairies, creatures that flit with the clever birds and expansive trees of a kingdom they know and will soon abandon as they grow. From the deck where we sit watching our girls in the yard, we wave at neighbors who stroll up the alley. We can hear the horses down the hill from where our house is one in a cluster of homes near the power company headquarters. When the fire sirens go off in the town below, we hear the horses kicking in their stalls, their whinnies loud enough to be heard in the baby monitor. Those nights, we hear everything through those speakers, the breathing of the two girls, the noises of the house, the horses, the air that wanders through.

Sometimes we think we hear people passing in the alley, and because everyone knows the women move around in the dark, it is easy to tell ourselves it is them, and it is easier still to think that they pose no threat.

3.

The fire sirens are loud and calling what everyone already knows. A girl is missing again, another youngster about the age our girls are now, playing in a driveway and then gone, easily, quietly, suddenly, completely gone. Everyone knows the story and the mother, a teller at the bank. Everyone knows the father has lived elsewhere for a while now, knows the grandmother spreads rumors, works at the post office and opens the mail of people she doesn't like, keeps a gun under the seat of her minivan. Is a regular attendee of church, and lets everyone know it.

There are those who know for certain that it is the twins. That the twins had something to do with it. The girl wore pink, wore braids, was the fussy kind of prim little lady that the twins always talk over, the kind of girl they cross a picnic or a store to get to. Those who know the mother worry it is too easy to blame the twins, that people are missing the fact that it may be anyone. The grandmother and her friends proclaim loudly that it is some deviant boyfriend *their slut mother brought home*.

It's the grandmother's son, the girls' father, no one has seen.

Her son who came back from Iraq quieter and thinner than when he left, her son who hasn't held a job more than a few months, her son who was asked to leave a firing range when he tore up targets with a fully automatic AK. When he was a cook for a few weeks at Hartley's, he hit a waitress for dropping a bowl of soup on his leg, and later had not the words to describe what the police figured out he thought was a reflex. For him, pain was a lash, a trigger to something he had taken into himself and would let out when his vision turned to red. Her son joked once about the twins, how *some old dude could let those bitches in the house and have a little party.* The latest rumor is that he has left town, looking for work in Pittsburgh, calling his ex-wife every once in a while and yelling until, weeping, she slams the phone down again and again.

The pickups of the volunteers throw blue light on our houses as they scream past on the road or rumble and bang down the alley behind us. Their noise makes feedback in the baby monitors, left on from the night before. Our girls watch *Snow White* on DVD and eat mac and cheese. We stand by windows, turn on the scanner, listen to the AM station out of East Brady, listen to the theories about vengeful gods and the end of the world, and the tight voices of people afraid to talk about how little they know.

Later, when most everyone else is asleep and darkness lets us pretend to have a reprieve until morning, we walk the yard picking up toys. We both see the movement at the same time, see the shadows among the buildings, see the hunched forms that could be bears, could be raccoons, could be the twins. As if the night creatures are out considering the threats. The toys thud hollow into the buckets, their plastic cool and damp with dew.

The grass is shaggy and shadowed, rangy at the fence. More than a few garages and back buildings sport new spotlights triggered by movement. Some nights, when we can't sleep, we watch the different patterns that shifting lights make on our ceiling, knowing the night moves through and among us out there.

4.

Many are startled but few are surprised when the twins lead a little girl out into a field behind the Walmart just after dawn. We put our bags down, others stop getting out of their car, and across the lot people begin to drift toward the spectacle of the girl emerging from the woods. Her knees are cut up, and she shakes with fear or fatigue or hunger. The twins bob and shuffle beside her. The twins' hands shake and it is not clear if they are cold, as it is the first frost this morning, or if they are talking. The girl's face has a smear of blood across a cheek that is old enough to be rust colored. Two men from the loading dock hop down to the macadam, start to walk, then run to the girl. Crows burst out of the stubbled corn field before the woods, the only sharp black in a field silvered with dawn and frost.

Then two lot attendants pushing carts back to the store stop, leave the carts, and start running. Their radios crackle, fried with alarm. People stream out through doors, carts left half-full and askance in deserted aisles where the light is as even as industry. At first there is chatter and then it is quiet. So still that the only noise is the footfalls of the twins and the girl as they cross into the cut stubs of cornstalks, and the sobs as the girl falls forward into the hands of the first man to reach her. We cannot understand what the girl says. She cries too hard, too deeply.

The twins stand in the cornfield as the girl goes with the men. They remain long enough for someone to suggest they had taken her. Some argue, others agree, but no one sees who first throws a rock. But everyone sees it arc, the arm that threw it strong enough to hurl it high and long. It lands well short of the twins, kicking dust into the air with a skittering sound. Then another rock sails out, and another. Voices boil into rage, the parking lot clamors. More rocks sail and the twins turn and shuffle back toward the woods and it is only when an ambulance siren begins to creep over the noise does the crowd part, shift, and disperse—making room for the ambulance, making its way back into the store, making the town return to itself.

The station in East Brady tuts over the response of the crowd. The grandmother of the girl complains to the line of people at the post office that she wants to know why the girls' *slut of a mother* wasn't there when her baby came out of the woods. The manager of the Walmart has called corporate to send someone out to help them talk about why the first rock was thrown and what it meant. It is widely discussed how the girl's father is not around, hasn't shown up for work, appears to have abandoned his pickup outside a truck stop out by I79. The owner of Hartley's promises a month of dinners for anyone with information leading to an arrest.

We watch the papers for the twins, watch the alleys, watch the lights and the streets. We watch the men smoke in front of the American Legion, watch the ministers spell out their admonitions in plastic letters snapped onto the signboards in front of their churches. We watch the people on our street plastic their windows and stack their wood, chain and lock their trash cans, rake their leaves while looking at the trees, at the hills beyond, at the smoke rising sure and warm from every house closed against the cold settling in the fields.

5.

The twins return to haunt their winter abodes but find doors closed, managers crossing their arms in doorways, barn doors locked. The warmth of buildings disperses as quickly as the smoke shreds over the chimneys and peaked roofs. At night people hear them pull on barn doors, the creak of wood and the report when the planks bang and slap against their frames. They shuffle into diners and move toward restrooms, ball caps turning to watch them, until a woman in an apron as worn as her face turns them back, or when a man shaven with a high and tight gestures back to the street. At the Sheetz, the police check in once a day. The human services office tells people to send the women their way once again, but the twins never linger long enough to hear the message. And if they do, they never follow it. We hear they have not been to the Office on Aging this year, not to the Human Services Bureau, not even to the apartments near the hospital where in years past, they have found sympathy among the bent and slowed women who live there.

The found girl returns to kindergarten. The AM station in East Brady invites the grandmother to make her case one week before Christmas. The girl's mother gives notice at the hospital, and we learn she will move down to Pittsburgh to Greensburg, somewhere where there is more work, better schools, hers the familiar story that has unmade this town for going on thirty years.

On the shortest day of the year, a hunter marches from the woods and into Hartley's. His face is serious as a woodsman's axe and he asks the manager to call the police. He leads two troopers to the twins, stiff, frozen, on the shady side of a bank deep in the woods, past the power company building, past the right of way, almost to the radio tower. The troopers remove their hats and stand on the quiet ridge looking down at the bank and the glade at the base, at the little stream dropping through the rocks that, had they followed it, would have led them back to the Walmart. A farmer carts their bodies out on a bier drawn by a horse.

The tributes include the young girl's inexplicable and sweet drawing of Ronald McDonald praying, posted on an easel at the plain patch where they are laid to rest; a week of old-time gospel music on the AM station; free coffee from Hartley's for the men and women holding candles in the field where the girl was found; and scores of knitted mittens that start appearing tied to telephone poles, newspaper dispensers, parking meters, and other places that we know, even though nothing is said, we *know* were knitted for them.

We will learn years later that the girl remembers her father taking her, leading her out of her home, leading her to his truck, making her drink cocoa *to get ready for a long drive, you little shit.* He had meant to flee, stopped for a shot to steel himself, calm his nerves, and the girl, woozy, had staggered out of the truck, gotten lost in the dark, amid the sounds of crows and leaves and the skitter of the possums and raccoons. She imagined she was a princess running from a queen, that she was found curled beneath a tree, her head resting in the crook of a root.

She may tell how fairies found her, speaking a strange language and feeding her scraps of bread, keeping her warm through the night as they lay with her, smelling of fur and caves and holes in the leaves. She will recall how they worked their way through the woods for a day and a night until she recovered enough to know she was lost and could talk the women into taking her someplace she would be found. She thinks she remembers them saying, *we will take you to the castle.*

But for this winter, for the rest of its darkest days, the creatures of our alley trigger the garage and shed lights like starbursts, and our daughters tell us that the ghosts of the twins still live with us. They tell us they hear their spells, hear their language, and as they do, their hands are never still.

COMMUNION

We were on a blanket, your pap and I, and we were young then, still afraid. What comes after you can probably guess, a pretty girl like you. Pap brought wine, a surprise. It was the war and you just couldn't get wine. I had met him after church and my parents thought I had gone into town. But your pap— no little worry of sin could keep me away from him. No threat, though just that morning I had heard the word of the Lord loud and clear as if that preacher were talking straight to me. My daddy sat next to me very stiff when the preacher went off about being there for the boys and what it did and didn't mean. I felt red, a feeling that will push through a pew and into hell. But I didn't mind it. We left.

Later, on the blanket near the river, your pap he started to get fresh, and I was of a mind to let him. His hands were the run of something lovely, the start of what I knew I wanted to finish. He smelled like water. Like a clean room in a hotel, brighter than the grass, a great welcome. I worried someone would see us, then felt like I wanted them to, that this was for a world beyond here, beyond what we knew. I welcomed a sudden glimpse, as the sin begged to be witnessed, to make it clean.

Then he stopped. He had seen a rabbit earlier, then heard a snap. I realized only later how fortunate we ourselves had been not to step into a trap. Whosoever had laid the traps hadn't posted a warning for his lines. It was the war, after all. People needed food. The rabbit had hit the trap.

I will never forget then what he did. He stood, twisted the rabbit's head and, to my surprise, skinned it in a single pull. My mother had always used a knife. By and by he built a fire and that day in the field, I ate rabbit, drank water like it was new, consumed a witness to sin, felt new all over again.

BEAUTIFUL FOR A DAY

Marie had long ago memorized the lazy curve of the front path in her renowned father's gardens, how it wended its way through leaning stands of yarrow, sage, comfrey, sedges, and rudbeckia, how it drifted out of sight before a stone mask of Neptune, in which hornets each year attempted a hive, and how each year a summer evening would come when the plant forms were only suggestions of what the daylight would reveal, and at the end of the path the famed grower himself would stand, Jean Rene, visible only as a red smudge of face pointed into a dot of cigarette, and she would hear the spray of a hose, and know the next morning the hornets would be gone. She never figured that when the end came, she would find his body there, beneath Neptune's mask, a hornet making its way across her father's face, looking to see whether to nest behind the thick lenses of his glasses.

The day of Jean Rene's funeral feast at Le Petit Cuchon, Marie's cousin Hildie was only one of the dozens of relatives in their im-

mense extended family who slurred or bawled at the head of the
room, but she was the most memorable. Even by the standards
of a family given to revel in coarseness as a shield against death,
she was beyond, reading her bawdy *homage á Jean*, a lengthy bit
of doggerel which mused on the anatomy of the saints as they
may be perceived by the famous botanist and breeder now in
heaven checking everyone out. She read it in the only outfit she
owned that could be close to mourning black, a sheath dress,
charcoal, in a stretchy rayon blend that, while it did cover everything, only *just*. But it was her hair, bleached almost-white,
which to Marie seemed most offensive. Marie thought, *she's
lucky everyone's plowed.*

And everyone was, except Marie, only child of the deceased
and now left with no living parents, looking to just get through
the day among people who, despite bloodlines, effectively were
strangers, and to move on to business. Aside from the fact that
her father would never speculate on the "schlong of Saint Fran-
cis and the reason he prances," it was just rude to commemorate
the dead in such a way, especially, as Marie pointed out to Hildie
later, when he was so important due to the contributions his
work had made to ornamental horticulture and botany. Hildie
made a raspberry and announced that the university and the
grower's organizations would take care of the podium com-
memorations, and that Marie should lighten up and have a glass
of wine and speculate on some anatomy herself.

"Go get laid by a distant cousin," Hildie said. "All the men in
this family can cook, so you might get breakfast too."

"Don't be ridiculous," Marie said. "You know it's just *not* an
appropriate way to talk about him *at all*, let alone at his funeral."

The way Hildie shrugged, a sloppy drunk shiver, Marie wasn't even sure the woman understood what she said.

Her actions made no sense—the woman had been beloved by her father. And Marie knew she loved him in return. Hildie and Marie had grown up together, practically as sisters, Hildie and her mom living in one of the apartments at the back of Jean-Rene's farm, the girls running through the fields and greenhouses, making mixtapes, Hildie imitating Madonna however she could and Marie singing Stevie Nicks. Marie wrote off the hostility to stress, to mourning, to the ferocity of Hildie. They shared a first car, walked into one another's homes without restraint, imagined their futures together—but that was all long ago.

Maybe Hildie's flagrance had its place. After the poem and the endless line of chafing dishes, after the consolations and hankies and rosary beads from dozens of spinster fists, Marie felt like something—hell, maybe flesh, if that was called for, or different food, maybe even liquor. She imagined Jean Rene's face wrinkle into a laugh at the mention of liquor. He'd say *how does a French girl hold her liquor? By the ears.* But she needed more than jokes and gluttony. More than the Catholic celebration of death right on the heels of maudlin prayers said on your knees. Something beyond the endless grind of nothing that seemed to fill the days since she found her father. She decided, though, that it was best just to leave.

While looking for her purse, she had to dodge two different men, each alone and with a drink lolling in his hand, each with the look for love. On making it to the door, she smelled the air outside, fresh mulch mixed with the gasoline from the station across the street from the restaurant, and she wondered how anyone could eat after walking through that, after the horrid smells of all that processing, the pollution warmed by the sun into something thick and horrid. Her father never mulched his beds, never scattered any processed covering over his prized daylilies. He would use his own compost, his own leaves, grass clippings, but never something processed through a chipper. "You never know what Pollack tossed a cigarette butt or coffee cup into the chippers," he said. "You just never know. Those people are filthy and reek they do, of sausage."

To Jean Rene, no one had ever had it bad as the French. The Irish, the Italians, the Czechs and Ukrainians, and later the Dominicans, the Mexicans—in his personal view of history, none dealt with the level of persecution endured by the French. He would mutter endless diatribes on the subject while he potted rhizomes, the door to the potting area ajar to let the air in, his cigarette smoldering at the corner of his mouth, in the permanent and slightly yellowed corner. He would poke the soil down around the fleshy root, then smooth a handful over the top, spin it a half turn, knock it on the edge of the plywood potting table, and drop it perfectly into place on a nursery cart. As he did so, people would come and go from his unofficial office—buyers, students, other growers, family members, and they would talk with him, endure his misanthropy because, in spite of it all, to talk with Jean Rene was to encounter an energy that was contagious. One of the eulogists at the funeral mass, in fact, had said that Jean Rene could exasperate, but in doing so, fill those he touched with a resolve that was hard won anywhere else. A left-handed compliment, to be sure, but one which Marie found herself nodding to. Nothing like a bastard to get people moving.

When she was young, Marie had sat near the potting bench, as often playing with stones as reading a book. She had sometimes watched him talk to the men and women in the doorway, all of them dusty with earth or mulch, streaked in sweat, all of them laughing with her father, the caustic fellowship of Jean Rene's bench the reason they kept coming. That and the daylilies, the prizewinners. On days when she had listened closely to her father, which is to say, on those days when he had called to her in the monologue—"Marie? Eh? Did you hear what I am asking you a moment ago? Listening, eh? Silly girl."—on those days, she had learned all about the struggles of the French, working down from Quebec, and up from Maryland, shuffled into jobs as cooks, bakers, and gardeners, with, her father insisted, "none of the respect due a common dog, none of the listening to how we are good at things, certain things, you know."

Outside Le Petit Cuchon, stirred by unexpected warmth of the sun on the blacktop, Marie thought, *Good at death. The French, that's what they are, good at death. Eat and pray, eat and pray.* She considered calling Nevin, but he'd want to talk about her students and, while they were great kids, it wasn't the time. She thought of getting a cab to come get her, but figured that, while waiting, someone would come out and offer her a ride and the circumstances of the day would compel her to accept, and she'd be stuck in one of the enormous Cadillacs or Buicks that the old patriarchs loved to drive slowly around town. She started to walk down the street, then, hoping that no one would exit the restaurant and see her, and run to offer her a ride or, worse, slow down, with traffic backing up and honking at her as she stood there, sweating in a black cardigan and wool skirt, dressed too warmly for June, and they would lean over toward an open window to shout, "Get inside! Where is your sense walking when it could so suddenly rain?"

She reached to her purse for a Tic Tac and hit a zipper where no zipper should have been. She stopped, pulled the sides of the purse and looked into stuff very much not her own. Old movie stubs, three lipsticks, several parking tickets, and receipts from a number of stores. Hildie's purse, this was. She swore and turned back to the restaurant, cursing her cousin in a splendid internal rant.

Inside, she found Hildie wrapped around a disheveled man with smoker's teeth and a two-day beard. As Marie strode up to her, she swore she heard Hildie whisper to the man, *grab my ass and remind me I'm alive*. Marie almost grabbed the ass herself, partly to poke at the seamless rayon expanse, partly to remind the woman just where the hell she was, but mostly out of spite for Hildie's buying the same purse as her. And same earrings, and same suits, and on and on, despite Hildie's frequent assertions that Marie was lame.

Marie poked her in the shoulder instead.

Hildie spun around. "Marie? What are you *doing?*"

"I think you must have moved my purse," Marie said. She noted the smeared mascara under the lids of Hildie's eyes, and was a bit surprised.

Hildie put her hand on the man's chest and told him to wait, and as the two women headed to a table, Marie suppressed a grimace when the man began to grind his pelvis as though dry-humping air.

"Good thing you came back," Hildie said, forcing a laugh. "I have stuff in the purse. It may be important later." She grinned back at Marie, who stopped walking.

"Maybe you can give it a rest, just today?"

Hildie frowned and Marie thought she saw her lower lip

24

twitch, just once. But then, Hildie'd had a lot to drink, the twitch could have meant anything. "Tell you what, you butt out and go home or wherever it is you're going, and I will do what I want? Can we agree?"

Marie suppressed the growing knot in her throat. "Where is my purse?"

Hildie pointed. "On the table." She stepped aside, and as Marie leaned down to retrieve it from under a jacket tossed over the table, Hildie said, "Just because someone is dead doesn't mean everyone has to stop living."

"Whatever, Hil. It's just a little, I don't know, inappropriate? It's a funeral," she said. It would not do to rage at her here, so Marie turned and walked away as calmly as she could, knowing her cousin would dismiss her once again.

The next morning, while Marie sat at her father's kitchen table watching a spirea's branch tips sway as raindrops hit them, the conservatory called, anxious to begin the work of establishing the Gault library. They assured Marie of their sensitivity at this difficult time, but stressed to her that her work on the project and her cooperation might be just the things to make her grieving somewhat more bearable. They had clearly picked the most obsequious person on the faculty to make the call. His voice had thickened and modulated as though he drank corn syrup while talking, and while each sentence he uttered began in the guise of condolence, he would end his phrases with the call to work, to responsibility and, the most annoying, the call to fulfill her father's wishes in leaving a legacy. The only legacy, she wanted to remind this man, that Jean Rene Gault wanted to leave the world was a summer-long season of daylily blooms.

Her father was, to a degree, famous. The introduction of his breeding masterpiece, *Hemerocallis* 'Love Supreme' made him winner of the American Hemerocallis Society's coveted Stout Silver Medal award. It had been the first pink constant re-bloomer in the field, changing the hue of long-haul re-bloomers from the gold and yellow of 'Stella D'Oro' and Darrel Apps' 'Happy Returns' to pink, a soft shell-pink—the pink, he used to joke, of a young woman's bottom. Even more, the pink did not fade within the flower's throat—it stayed constant almost entirely down the neck, flushing green only at the deepest part, from which the stamens thrust, ending in Dayglo yellow. The propagation ban lifted only a year ago, and growers were starting to sell fans to would-be daylily tycoons, and with the penchant for selling near-misses or otherwise corrupted plants, there was now great interest in housing the texts and notes that went into building the plant that would very likely sweep more awards and become as important an ornamental staple as the *Echinacea purpurea* cultivars or *Coreopsis verticillata* 'Moonbeam.'"

She assured the man that she would begin the process of boxing and categorizing books, and that she would contact the offices at the week's end, giving her enough time to get a good handle on what actually existed in the library, and whether any texts would warrant special consideration due to rarity or other factors. She had to admit, by the end of the conversation, what had originally seemed to her an interminable stretch of a morning had attained a definition and purpose. While it would be difficult to go through her father's things, she would have a mission which would distract her, and work which would make her feel productive. What a fitting way to honor him, she thought, with work.

She could not shake the image of his reedy frame, bagged over with chambray shirts and faded Dickies, standing in a column of smoke and soil dust, one hip leaning into the potting bench, his fingers poking away at soil or brushing vermiculite back into a tub or simply gathering pieces of leaves and rhizomes to compost. To the conservatory, such an image was probably their idea of the professor at work, but to her, this was the father in his home amid the palpable smells of soil and water, roots and smoke, humid moss and sun and the waning morning smell of onions in an iron skillet.

All those smells came back to her when she entered his study. Even her coffee could not overpower it. She put the mug down on the corner of the library table, an enormous piece occupying the middle of the second-floor room. On it, organized into stacks which did not, unfortunately, reveal much about their deceased owner's plans for them, lay dozens of books and magazines, papers and reports, all in some way linked to the project that had been Jean Rene's life work. She lifted the front page of one, the title of which included phrases like "microrhiza proliferation" and "tertiary root development." Next to it, overflowing, an ashtray of clay, with sides fashioned to resemble daylily roots. She had always been surprised at the hidden world of botanical knick-knacks, and here yet was another, one that, in all of her life near her father, she had never seen.

She looked up, scanning the shelves and prints and the riot of pothos, orchids, and cacti near the window, and felt as though she would drop through the floor. She wanted help, and the urge to call out hit her like a sudden wind, but when she went over options about whom to call, the idea seemed more and more hopeless. Despite their willingness and friendliness, she did not think she could trust the conservatory to represent her best interests. The man, Malcolm, came off well enough, but she had inherited Jean Rene's distrust of just about everything, and so he would not do. She thought fleetingly of her colleagues, but she did not know what she would encounter in the collection, what item would freshen the wound, stagger her out of the blur that pillowed her now, and scrape the death back to her, make her break down. Reluctantly, she began to concede that it would have to be family and, like it or not, probably Hildie.

She picked up the daylily ashtray and took it to the trash can to empty it, and as she turned it over, was surprised to see it inscribed to her father on the back, from Andrea, and dated 1985. She remembered Andrea then, though no one other than Jean Rene had ever called her that. The boys on the crew called her Brutus because, despite being only five feet and wisp thin, she could lift and move balled trees, split grasses with her hands, throw hay bales and mulch bags as far as any of them. All that strength but with pretty white skin and a bow mouth. And, it turns out, an apparent ability with clay.

Marie remembered liking her and hating the men who called her Brutus, even though Andrea seemed to revel in it. She just didn't remember any of the help having such a relationship with her father that they would want to fashion handicrafts for him. Then again, he was always at the nursery or in the beds in back, always with his crews, so who knew what sorts of loyalty he inspired there? Even at the potting bench, everyone seemed the same with him, like old friends, all buoyant in his loud attention. On the rare Sunday, usually in winter, when he would take her for an omelet, or accompany her and her late mother to church, Marie was always astonished at the number and variety of people who said hello to him, how many faces took on warmth as he approached. She was the more surprised because she did not have any romantic illusions about him; he was a son of a bitch to just about everyone. Jean Rene's wit was caustic, and he seldom knew when to reign it in, and yet, outside of the gardens, people went out of their way sometimes to cross a street or jog across a parking lot just to say hello to him. Perhaps, she thought, it was because he was the kind of son of a bitch who would smile so fully when he told you to fuck off that you'd always assumed he was just being a card. She thought of Hildie—smiles seemed to get her a long way.

They were ridiculous, the two of them.

She put the ashtray back on the table, inhaled deeply while running a hand down her stomach, and picked up the phone to call Hildie. It occurred to her then that she at least owed Nevin a call, to let him know the likely timeline of her return, so that he could in turn inform her students. She knew the substitute they were to be stuck with, a dilettante whose wife owned a number of area restaurants, the type of man she suspected looked at a high school biology class as an opportunity to watch girls all day. His bearing and presence reminded her of her own chemistry instructor in her first college lab. He would shimmy the spaces between the closely spaced lab tables, rubbing himself on the girls as he passed. More than once, Marie was aware he was aroused, and tried in vain to press herself through the slate tables and away from him, and could never understand why some of the girls giggled about it later. It was nothing to giggle about. But to some, of course, he had been handsome, in a rugby team kind of way, and he had worn just enough cologne to be effective (that much she had to admit), but the impropriety, the assumption of it all bothered her, and she hoped that she would make it back to her charges before the round of labs she had scheduled prior to the Easter break.

It hit her then that she would not have the genetics field trip this year, and that her students would not experience her father's lucid and entertaining lecture and demonstrations about hybridization. They would not force their own fingers to push into daylily roots, would not attempt their own crosses, their own quickie tissue culture. No six-foot hoagie in the back yard while she watched Jean Rene's face twist with the desire for a cigarette, and no shouting match later when she learned he had smoked with a few students behind the woodpile. Even dead he could be exasperating.

She cut the thought short, and called Hildie, knowing that first things come first.

Hildie, thank god, was not there when Marie found the Polaroids. Having announced that she needed a break from the dust, Hildie offered to get Marie and herself some lunch, and Marie assented, even though it probably meant Hildie would return with something like burgers and beer. Marie forgot all of it when she had unshelved some books and discovered one was hollow on its inside. Jean Rene had carved a space in the pages of an old copy of *Hortus Third* and inside the hollow were around two dozen Polaroids of young women variously undressed, all cheerfully debased in front of the camera which she only doubted for a moment could have been held by her father. In that moment, she speculated that they were little more than dirty pictures he had obtained somewhere, but then she noticed one was Andrea, and then another was Karen, a big-boned Italian girl who had been an intern from Del Val nearly a decade ago. Then she recognized another, an aspiring florist named Wendy, and before long, she realized they were all young women who had, at one time and however briefly, worked at the daylily farm, all in close quarters with her father, and all of them had chosen to undress for him for whatever reason.

She noticed her hands trembled, and she put down the photo tried to stop the trembling. She looked down and saw the harsh white glare of a girl's breasts, and turned the photos over. Then she shoved them all quickly back into the book and re-shelved it. She crossed the room, sat in his desk chair, but could not take her gaze from the spine of the book. *Hortus Third*, she thought, *Hurt Us, Whore Us, Here Us, hear us?* Some of those girls had actually babysat her, or had made her dinner when her parents were running late at a trade show or a supplier's. Some of those girls had acted as her friends.

She heard Hildie's voice, from the funeral, with that awful poem, another of its lines, *ask for a toot on the root, zee jizz-ohm de rhizome.* She wondered what Hildie saw in Jean Rene that she could ascribe to his departed character such lines, such perception. How did she miss it? How did his own daughter and frequent partner miss this other existence, this side of her father? She wasn't stupid. She knew of his other vices. Perhaps, with this one, with all the social taboos it violated, given the age of some of the girls, he was simply extra careful. It surprised her to think of her father being aware of guilt, of transgression, since so many of his other vices he celebrated with near aban-don. Or, at least, with no hint of apology.

She surveyed the rest of the books, and realized she would have to look through every shelf. Flip through every book. What else might be squirreled away in the gutted innards of old botany texts? What had her hoary, caustic father shoved into books to hide from those who legitimately loved him? And now, she couldn't really have any more help. It would have to be her. No archivist or museum person could be allowed to stumble upon anything, and Hildie, certainly, would have to go, or be more controlled. She saw the weeks of afternoons spent in this room, and then in the greenhouse, then Sunday mornings spent cleaning out the office at the back of the gardens. She had lived two thirds of the man's life with him, and now she would live with him after death, with the remnants of his soul and all its shadows, and now she knew her work was to protect him. It was a protection he would neither have wanted nor expressed any gratefulness for, but it was a protection she would provide, for no better reason than that he was her father, and she wanted to give his name and his work that protection, to gird his research with the dignity such endeavors deserved and inspired. But then, who was she kidding? She could hear Hildie upbraiding her for such sanctimonious views. As if the Curies never stole a glance or a grab in the lab. As if all that thinking and probing didn't lead people to think about a little probing. Now she was even thinking in the sorts of wordplay in which Hildie would take lascivious delight.

She started to wonder who, of the girls she could remember, was *not* among the photos. At first, she simply wanted some assurance that her father had not, indeed, slept with all of them— yes, she knew, it wasn't clear whether he actually did, but there's not much to do after you talk girls into splaying themselves before the camera lens of their boss, so the likelihood was there. If he had not, it would somehow affirm for her that his pursuit of them at least had some criteria, and he was not terribly crazed. Or not as crazed as some kind of predator. Her face grew hot at the thought of such equivocation. She pulled the book back down and flipped through the photos as fast as she could, working to keep her eyes on their faces, however difficult it was at times, given some of the poses. When she was through, she was surprised at how uncertain she was, how many faces she must have forgotten. She didn't know why, but she felt as though, by forgetting, she was betraying them at the moment.

To Marie's surprise, Hildie returned with salads and diet soda. "If we're working all afternoon, we don't want anything heavy, right?"

Marie nodded, still a little jittery from the photos, and quickly spirited the hollow book and its contents into her backpack. She felt as though Hildie could read the deception on her face, then told herself Hildie would not be able to tear her thoughts away from her own fabulousness long enough to notice anything about Marie.

They sat, dressed their salads in silence, opened their sodas, and as Marie was about to fork at her greens, Hildie leaned back dramatically against the lower shelves.

"So, I didn't tell you about my disastrous night yet, did I?"

Marie looked at her cousin for a moment, then proceeded to work at her salad, as she would be doing a lot of listening.

"Didn't think so," Hildie said. "So after the dinner, the other night—"

"After the funeral," Marie said.

Hildie smirked. "Yes, whatever, after the *funeral*. After the funeral, I accepted a ride home with this guy, Louis, I think he must be a second cousin. One of *ma tante* Juliet's grandchildren. Sweet man. Knew how to dance."

Marie couldn't resist, even though her mouth was too full of spinach. "The guy I saw you dancing with? The pelvis?"

"No. No, not him," Hildie said. "Different one."

Marie shrugged. Hildie took the gesture as the starting gun, and as Marie slowly finished her salad, Hildie detailed how she had looked forward to seeing this Louis undressed, and yet when they arrived at her apartment, he began to tell her about his previous lives, how he practiced Wicca, and how he was suspicious of the motives of his lesbian roommate. "I was like, *and all this is apropos of what?* And he was like, we're talking, right?" Long story short, Hildie said, though it was not short, was that he left, and there was no fun to be had by all. Those were the words she used. Marie put her salad down and regarded her cousin.

"You didn't find anything wrong with, you know, trying to seduce family?"

Hildie chewed an enormous bite of salad, swallowed hard, and said, "Family. What is that? And how close can he possibly be? I mean, our grandmother was the twelfth of fifteen kids. Each of those kids had about three kids apiece, and then those kids, *our parents*, had three or four each. We number in the hundreds. We're pretty thinned out. Hell, I bet the statistics are pretty good that, if we live near the bulk of our family like we do, odds are we've dated someone who's a blood relative, however little of that blood we may share."

"That is a bullshit rationale," Marie said. "And I don't know about your statistics, there, Hil. Have you ever worked with statistics?"

"I sell tea," she said, "The only statistics I care about are closing averages."

Marie wanted to point out that percentages were not necessarily statistics, but she could feel herself on the verge of being exactly the kind of person Hildie always accused her of being. She took a sip of soda.

"Well, do what you want, I guess," Marie said, trying to sound flip.

"I will. Thanks for the permission."

They were quiet for several moments, the only sound that of Hildie chewing.

"So I think I have a system for how we can make progress with these books," Marie said. "I will take the books off and put them in piles, you can box them and label them. Then, we can both move them to three piles, one for the library, one for us, and one for yard sale. Sound good?"

Hildie nodded, then gestured with her fork. "Watch it as you un-shelve them," she said. "You know, some of them have shit stuffed in them."

Marie felt a flush shoot down her neck.

"What?"

Hildie put down her fork, straightened her back, stretched. As she returned to her salad, she said. "You know, he hollowed out some of the books, kept shit in there, cash, letters, other stuff he didn't want anybody to find."

"Like what else?"

Hildie looked at her, worked at her teeth with her tongue. After making a brief sucking sound, she said, "Didn't you know he did that?"

Marie didn't know whether to say yes or no.

"You didn't, then," Hildie said.

Marie shook her head.

Hildie nodded, and Marie could see she was thinking about where to start. Marie thought, *how about the obvious?*

"How is it that you know?" Marie asked.

"I'm a snoop," Hildie said, matter-of-factly. "I have always loved to come up here and read, and when Mom and I lived in the apartment out back after my dad left, I used to come up here and read all the time." She waved at Marie, "You were in college, no one else seemed to be around, I wasn't quite dating yet, so I'd come up here and read. One day I was looking around, and I pulled out a book, and plop, out drops a bag of weed."

Marie had forgotten that little period in Jean Rene's history. The few times she saw him with the thin smoke, she thought it was just another kind of cigarette until she went to her first frat party. God, she'd been sheltered.

"So, I started looking around every chance I got," Hildie said. "He had all sorts of shit in here. He was quite the operator," Hildie said.

"So you knew."

Hildie said, "About the weed—?"

"No, the pictures."

"Huh? Pictures?"

"The girls. He took pictures of them."

Hildie looked away, and Marie saw her suppress a grin.

"It's not funny, Hil. It's fucking, it's just—it's ridiculous and it's wrong."

"Calm down, Marie, what kind of pictures are we talking about?"

"Polaroids. You know. The kind of thing you didn't send off to Fotomat back in the day."

Hildie nodded. "Well, I didn't realize he was doing that. But come on, the way he was with everybody, you can't be surprised."

"What do you mean *the way he was with everybody*?" Marie could hear her cracks starting in her voice and she wanted very much to fight it.

"Well, he—I just knew that he, and some girls, sometimes, were flirty, and then it sometimes got carried away. It never lasted."

"Clearly."

Hildie put a hand on Marie's arm. "Come on, you *knew* he wasn't perfect. This can't be that big a surprise for you."

Marie's eyes began to sting, and she willed herself to hold it together. "I'm not kidding, I don't know why it is, but I've really only *just* found out." Marie pressed the flat of her hand against her forehead. "He wasn't your father, you know? That makes a difference."

Hildie's face hardened. "Yeah, you know, you're right, he wasn't *my* asshole father, he wasn't the guy who left and fucked us over and damn near killed my mom. Yeah, he wasn't my father, but he was the only man who ever really meant anything to me close to what a father is."

"Stop being melodramatic," Marie said. "I'm not saying he's a bad man. It's just a lot to process."

"Whatever," Hildie said. "Just don't treat him like a fallen saint. It's kinda offensive."

"Fine." Marie sat for a moment. "How many? How many knew?"

"A lot of people knew, Marie. All the girls, obviously. A lot of the growers around here," she said. "I heard about it from people, joking about him. I didn't appreciate it, but what could I do?" She looked at her hands. She knew then that Hildie was stalling, avoiding telling her what she now suspected, that her mother knew, and did nothing. That the whole time, her mother had allowed it all to go on, for whatever reason never saying anything to her husband, or anyone else, about it. When Hildie finally inhaled, steeling herself to say it, Marie interrupted.

"So, my mother knew as well, then."

"Yeah."

Marie felt her eyes begin to sting. She was not going to do this here. "Why the hell couldn't I have figured it out? If it was so obvious, why didn't I figure this out? How in the hell did *you* figure it out?"

When Hildie looked up, Marie saw her eyes glisten, and felt her stomach drop.

"Not you. No. Not you."

Hildie shook her head. "He tried, asked, maybe, I don't know. He didn't come out and say it, but he looked at me once. I don't know how to explain it. You know how when a man is going to kiss you he gets a look? You know that look? All intent, kind of almost desperate? You know that look? He gave it to me once."

Marie ran a hand through her hair. She wondered if, indeed, she did know that look.

"Nothing happened, and he never did it again, I never did anything, said anything," Hildie said. She brought her knees up. "I know it doesn't sound like such a big deal, I mean, worse things have happened to people. But I was so surprised. It just bowled me over, floored me. It's like I saw him weak, and despite how annoying he could be, I never thought of him as weak."

"Neither did I," Marie said, before she realized what she said.

At the end of two days, Marie realized she was snapping at Hildie

38

nearly every time she spoke. Hildie, to her credit, endured much of it in silence, but a silence punctuated by eye rolling, buried sighs, boxes left in the way, and other minor signs of annoyance. Marie supposed Hildie was feeling an altruistic streak, as much as she could, and chose not to say anything directly, to let her cousin mourn her father all over again, but to let her know she wasn't pleased about the crappy attitude. By the end of the second day, at the rear of the back garden, over glasses of wine and crossed arms, the two decided a helper was needed, and that Hildie could return to her work, guilt-free, knowing she had done her part.

Hildie's suggestion came, actually, somewhat inadvertently, out of the discussion that drew them to the garden in the first place. They had ended for the day, and as they noticed the night-opening daylilies stretch their blossoms in the back garden, they speculated on how to handle that season's upcoming crop of divisions. Hildie joked about the boys from the work study office at Del Val, and while her cousin had a vision of sweaty young men glistening before her, Marie saw neutral, skilled, strong people to help categorize, box, and carry books as she took them from shelves. It was perfect. One boy (or girl, even) boxing and moving would handle only books she had gone through herself, and would then help her with some of the heavier work, some of the drudgery, and she could devote herself wholly to the organization and general assessment of the library. It would get Hildie off the hook, a hook Marie felt Hildie hung herself upon because of pieties of family and duty. This would allow her a guiltless Get Out of Jail Free card.

Still, Hildie smirked when she showed up the first Saturday and found Marie working with Terrence. Terrence graduated the month before and was bound for Penn State in the fall, to pursue a degree in ornamental horticulture. Marie had let him hang out in her labs, helping younger students, when he had his study halls, and for as long as Marie had known him, he had worn gray t-shirts and a high-and-tight haircut. When she inquired once what the boy's parents did, she was surprised neither was in the military. This, then, was Terrence's bearing, gray t-shirt and buzz cut, quiet but for the occasional please and thank you.

But, as Hildie pointed out, he was also an eighteen-year-old man. *All that stamina,* she'd said, *can be put to better uses than boxing books.* Marie figured she was feeling better because she actually laughed when Hildie said that. They could hear Terrence upstairs, books thunking into boxes, tape ripping out to seal the tops. Marie was supposed to be getting him a drink, but she was instead laughing in her kitchen, and Hildie seemed, unusually, to not be annoying her.

"Are you sure you don't want me to help?"

"Positive," Marie said. "This way you're not mired in here."

"I can see why you don't want me around," Hildie said, "Was that boy on the swim team or something? Did you see his chest?"

"I don't know," Marie said. She could feel Hildie pushing it. If they were to part amiably, she'd have to go soon.

"Hmmm. Well, do you at least need my truck when it comes time to move things?"

"That might be good," Marie conceded.

"He helped me buy that truck, you know," Hildie said. She looked at her feet. The hoop earrings flashed with sun, as if she were slightly reverberating. "He went to the dealer with me, and yelled the guy down on the price. When the brakes went a week later, he sent the guy a fruit basket. All lemons. They fixed the brakes the day they got the basket."

They were quiet. Above, Terrence thudded away.

"Your dad was a sonovabitch," Hildie said, trying to smile. Marie thought she looked pretty, even as her eyes—too made up for a Saturday morning—glistened. *She shouldn't try so hard*, she thought, *but all she does is try hard.*

"He certainly was," Marie said, thinking, *you don't know the half of it.* The Polaroids flashed in her mind, and she knew to get upstairs before Terrence started freelancing. She walked Hildie to the door, and as she watched her drive away, she saw the first bloom of Jean Rene's sentimental favorite, a daylily not his own, but one he loved for its tidiness. It had opened far at the end of the front beds, the winey-purple trumpet of 'Little Grapette,' thrusting out from a low line of daylilies. She had almost forgotten it was June, but of course, here it was, and her father, in the ground, missed the year's first cups on his favorite flower, those blossoms that only stayed while the sun did. She inhaled, but the breath caught in her and she held the doorjamb while she coughed her breathing back to normal.

When she returned to the library, having brought a bottle of water for Terrence, she saw he'd finished the boxes, had taped and labeled everything, and was regarding the shelf on which she'd stopped. As she entered the room, he reached for the books, and Marie strode to him and touched his arm, just stopping herself from grabbing it more forcefully. His skin was cool, the hair on his arm surprisingly soft, and she could smell soap on him, something very rough and unperfumed, but clean. She let her hand remain on his arm maybe a bit too long, but she explained it quickly.

"It's just, these are my dad's books, and I really wanted to go through each one myself," she said. She looked away from him, at the boxes. "I appreciate your help, I do, I just, well, do you understand?"

"Yes, I do," he said. He looked right at her, as though surprised to find her as close as she was. "Just let me know what you want me to do."

She'd known this boy since she'd started teaching, just four years ago, right after her master's degree. He had been recommended to her for after-school activities, had gone on trips to Jean Rene's gardens, had led a biology study group at the school, and had been in all ways a responsible, reasonable, thoroughly unusual young man.

He backed away from her a step, looked at her hand, still on his arm, and then at her face. Marie focused on his lower lip, the pink of it, the hue of Love Supreme, Jean Rene's most famous creation. But here, in this man's mouth, the hue stayed all pink, all softness, all depth of a momentary and surprising beauty. Looking at him, she saw her father, in all his frailty, all his worn desire, and all that must have shimmered before his eyes, all the beauty he had never fully accepted as fleeting, knowing from his work that beauty only lasts a day, and that you can never hold it, try as you might.

Pick Up

You sit in your pick-up truck, outside the restaurant, trying to be absorbed in your copy of *Foreign Affairs*, afloat in a space of puddles and bumper stickers. You wear a sport coat, the back of its collar worn near-white, and the hem of it out by your left thigh. Under the coat, a red t-shirt, and you wear thin khakis and work boots. In the restaurant, your daughter has last bits of salad and last words for the week with her mother. You have before you a weekend of infinite pauses and a looming job interview, about which you can only worry. Into this your daughter will step, your diffuse existence, your trap of contradictions, you without cable, no snacks in the house, no phone other than your cell. You who can barely keep alive the potential for her continued visits, you to whom the judge referred to as being "in a rebuilding phase."

You remember last night's PBS special on Yalta—Stalin's smirk frozen in the documentary's final frame, that enigmatic expression. Stalin wasn't the enigma, it was the moment they

43

framed. Was it Stalin himself, horribly cognizant of all to follow, happy at circumstances spreading before him like treasure? Or was he mugging for the cameras—and the accident of timing and hindsight combine to force you again to that image? The three of them—they thought they'd set the world in their image. Roosevelt had his chin up, as though fighting to lift himself to his feet. Churchill looked squashed. Were they faces of consciousness, horrible awareness, or just a trick of light? Or have their faces taken the shape of what we know now?

You see your daughter waiting to cross the street. A truck slows and the two men inside—your age, laborers—turn their heads to rub their eyes over her. You see how they see her, the curve of her calf below the short skirt you hate, the front of her pushed into an offering. But it's her face that makes you gape. They pass her, and while she doesn't look at them, you know she saw them. And you can't yet tell if what lurks in her eyes is weariness, sorrow, or pleasure, what thing makes her lids heavier in the dim light afforded by winter's clouds, what arrests you. As she steps off the curb, it's gone. You see her eyelashes against her cheeks, her mother's walk in every step. You see how she comes closer but never near, how she will get in the truck and you will treat her wrong, all weekend, in your stubborn insistence that she is a girl in your image.

Nguyen Van Thieu is Dead at 78

Nguyen Van Thieu, the former president of South Vietnam, is dead at age 78. He kept his firewood neatly stacked, and his porch was always clean. The crispness about his home made ours appear slovenly, at the edge of acceptability in this neighborhood of so many Volvos and well-heeled golden labs. To me, Nguyen Van Thieu was simply Ng, the guy who wore shorts nearly every day when the weather was warm, and who, when he did venture out for fish or cigarettes, rode a bike, and never on the sidewalk, always on the road. Nguyen Van Thieu had a wife, I believe—that is, he lived with a woman I assumed was his wife—but she was a person who was only heard, seldom seen. The wife of Nguyen Van Thieu was a breeze of piano notes, a low rumble of the dryer and the smell of fabric softener, or the occasional Olds Cutlas Sierra that backed out of her garage as slowly as I have ever seen a car deliberately move.

I did not, at first, make it a habit to watch the home of Nguyen Van Thieu. I had far more interest in the tumult across the street, the Filipino couple and their six children, all teenagers or older—the regular comings and goings, well into the nights I couldn't sleep, when I would watch their daughters extricate themselves carefully from dates and eager boyfriends. Houses are close in Foxboro, and one knows much about a neighbor through simple proximity. But then, one also knows little. The Filipinos were to me, obvious and chaotic children, and once I lost interest in their predictable affairs, I started to watch our silent neighbor.

He was never quite furtive, but it seemed he was more reticent than most of the people who kept to themselves. His name led me to guess he was Vietnamese, but his appearance gave me doubt: he was well-fed, with an almost youthful shine to his features, the crispest of haircuts. Such clues were baseless, I knew, and I also understood that most of my associations with Vietnamese were limited to being in-country, and seeing far more disheveled and desperate faces.

To watch Nguyen Van Thieu, I had to move my chair, away from the bed, closer to the window and at an angle, so that every time I looked into his yard, it was obliquely. My looking revealed little. After the accident and Clara's injury, after what I saw, I took all that I knew about Nguyen Van Thieu and placed it in the front of my head each night for several weeks, wondering about him, about how we all got here—him, my son and daughter-in-law, my granddaughter, all of us—to a moment of such great pain in our house. Despite my watching and all the time I devoted to it, I still knew little.

For instance, I learned only a few days ago that my neighbor was the former president of South Vietnam. What I did know: Nguyen Van Thieu enjoyed strolling onto his porch in the evenings and belching, apparently under the delusion that no one could hear him. This delusion was fostered no doubt by the row of hemlocks, clipped and austere, that separated our yards.

I often wondered what Nguyen Van Thieu could hear me do. Our bathroom window overlooked his back yard, and so I was sure to close it whenever I entered that room with reading material, so as not to offend the ears of Nguyen Van Thieu.

We never heard those television-humor sounds omnipresent in the fictional suburbs of sitcoms coming from the house of Mr. and Mrs. Nguyen Van Thieu, nor any acrobatic panting of their making love. We never heard dramatic screams between the two of them, or children sassing back. As far as we knew, there were no children, never a sign of them—never, in that yard, was there a tricycle overturned or a ball sad and disconsolate near the road edge. Never did the yard of Nguyen Van Thieu resemble ours.

Nguyen Van Thieu, the former leader of communist resistance and friend to Henry Kissinger, loved to watch soccer on cable. Often the volume was turned up so loud it was as if the match were being played among the hemlocks that separated our yard. Nguyen Van Thieu must have had a high-quality television with excellent speakers, because the voices moved among the hemlocks like wood thrushes, deft and hidden.

In the silence that had descended upon our home in the last few years, our ears sought the comfort of other sounds, some ratification of existence elsewhere, and the voices of soccer matches grew ever more specific to me, more recognizable. Now

47

that Nguyen Van Thieu is dead at age 78, and his widow has, by all indications, left the house—perhaps to return to the denser air of her childhood home; their lawn will surely grow unruly soon—I will probably listen for sounds even farther from here.

Sound was, for a long time, all I knew about the accident. Visual memory I have had to build myself.

I remember hearing their garage door go up, since it so seldom did. Clara must have made noise while playing, and I might have even known she was there, but the constancy of her play was such that I rarely realized I heard her. I do remember my son saying her name over and over, and not knowing why. I made it to the window to see him lift her and hold her, her head lolling back to reveal the raw white of her neck. Her limbs were caught in a crush of spasms.

What came next I know: he drove her to the hospital, both because it was close and because it takes ambulances too long to arrive in our neighborhood. We know it might have aggravated damage, we know about the possibilities of further harm, but he could not have done any differently. It is simply the way he is.

The night of the accident, I heard my son's car pull into the port, and I went downstairs to talk with him. He did not come in to the house. Instead, he stood near the hemlocks, watching the spot on the sidewalk, watching for a long time before he let his face fall into his hands.

From what we have been able to get from Clara, we understand that the car hit her tricycle as she was pedaling after a ball. Nguyen Van Thieu's drive is sloped, and so even when the car hit her and braked, it still rocked back a good way. Clara was hit once, and she fell violently to the sidewalk. But the car, in rocking to a stop, pushed the tricycle, and Clara, farther, and she jolted off the curb, hitting her head again on the street. It was so sudden and brutal that she never screamed, and her cries afterward were hoarse, catching in her throat, as if they were too much to heave out at once.

Clara injured her head in a way the doctors described as shaking and bruising the brain. While there was not much exterior damage to her head, the force it endured was enough. She was left with motor control problems which would only be overcome with extensive—and expensive—therapy.

We became fluent in the continents of the brain, with the anterior cingulate cortex and the cerebral cortex, with all the connections her doctors knew little about beyond the damage and what was affected. It struck me how fully they understood the limits of their knowledge, and how difficult it must be to traffic in that which is not understood. We were entangled in the same struggle. No one but Clara and Nguyen Van Thieu's wife saw what happened; neither of them saw completely, and neither is talking.

There are many things we could have done differently, my son says. We could have required her to play in the backyard. We could have been closer to her. We could have made her wear her helmet even on short rides rather than give in to her whining. Because he is in pain, I resist telling him of the futility of hindsight. I resist telling him how second thoughts have dominated my life, and how I do not want them to dominate his, even though they will. There will be time for such realizations later.

The oddest fact about the days following the death of Nguyen Van Thieu was that no one came to the house. I grew quite certain his widow had left. Not once was there a caller, and yet newspapers did not pile up. It was as though the world had accepted this, or knew and expected it, and no one had been left uninformed. Even the grass, which should have grown shaggy and shadowy beneath tufts of crabgrass and the first descending leaves, acted as though it had received the message to grow more slowly, and decided to obey. When it rained this morning, the puddles at the end of his drive, near our mailbox, were colorful where the oil floated, oil that had remained on the surface of his new driveway: at last, a sign that Nguyen Van Thieu did not in fact control the world.

We all knew Nguyen Van Thieu didn't control the world, didn't we? Where was he when that last Huey Hogg left Saigon and the people clawed each other out of the way to get at the struts underneath that bobbing copter, some falling off like bits of food from the great mouth of an emperor in retreat? Where was he on that final day—long since fled from the patch of a country we loosely and impermanently thought of as his? Those of us who were there, anywhere in that crescent of desolation, in that awful and murderous jungle, remember the smell, the rot and stink of sweat, the countryside and the blasted smell of char, and beyond that, the aroma of so much gone so wrong.

Nguyen Van Thieu did not smell it, but neither was he yet belching in Foxboro or barbecuing or watching soccer matches. He was perhaps in Brussels, sating himself on chocolate smoother than any silk he had ever encountered, glossy cameos of white chocolate like Jacquard, toffee like milk glass. Or maybe he had made it as far as Paris or London, dining secretively on fat anchovies and crusty bread, hunkered in cheap apartments among Chinese and Koreans who had fled earlier wars. He could have arrived in Taiwan through any number of circuitous routes. However he traveled then, he did not want to be known. He was still at least two homes away from Foxboro, from the most anonymous country in the world. He still had eight lives left, an easy metaphor for a complicated retreat, but one I cannot help thinking about, especially when I see him, as I will always see him, running to the side of that behemoth automobile as the door swings open to his hand, his wife's slippered foot trembling toward the pavement.

He only thought of her, only wanted to be near her. On one level I understand the impulse, given all that he had seen and led and known about, given what he must have remembered about fragility. But I can't forgive Nguyen Van Thieu or his wife for not helping Clara. I can't forgive the cowardice that, at the time, I thought I recognized.

Each winter, Nguyen Van Thieu first delighted in the snow and then cursed it. When he used a snow blower he would yell, believing no one heard him over the engine's noise. I now realize Nguyen Van Thieu's cursing when he thought he could not be heard was a metaphor constructed like a snowflake, the most fragile crystalline connections put together in the cold. There are many ways to read it.

Much about Nguyen Van Thieu remains distant from me, but this is the biggest question: how could Nguyen Van Thieu persist in telling the police that he did not see the accident happen? Nguyen Van Thieu did see it. Otherwise why was he so quick to come to his wife in the driveway? Why then did he not come to help? Why did he not wince at the sight of Clara and the terrible flopping of her arm as my son lifted her? Had he become so inured to suffering that this girl failed to move him in her pain?

Nguyen Van Thieu possessed an enormous parka, filled with down, probably the largest piece of clothing he had ever owned, an utter oddity in the steam of his former home. He would wear it while standing in his backyard watching the squirrels skitter through the hemlocks. He resembled a solitary bullet, erect in the snow in the shining gray fabric of his parka.

The squirrels are ungoverned. They are capitalists. They keep and keep and gather and gather, and do not worry about who has given and who still needs. They answer to no one, no international influence, no business cartels, no puppet governments. They do not worry about committees and imperialism and taking measures. Nguyen Van Thieu watched them, and I wondered what he could be thinking. It is of course ludicrous to assume, just because I have new information about the life our neighbor used to have, that he was a man continually preoccupied by the ghost of his position as head of an embattled and disappearing state. It may well be that he seldom reflected on what he had left behind, or the images from afterward, the skulls as plentiful as rice grains. I believe that he could have had thoughts that were utterly chaste because he was capable of emptying his mind when it came to a little girl. He stood like a bullet, loaded, volatile, and silent, harmless without the gun, the hammer, the state. Contemplating hemlocks.

Each time a car comes slowly down our street—especially if it happens to be a large sedan, or of a dark color—I wonder if it contains some emissary of the departed Nguyen Van Thieu. If I am outside I try to remember the smell of their home, whether I ever sensed anything on the breeze, something that made it through the hemlocks, something like the biting smell of kim-chee that comes every so often from my backyard neighbors or the acrid jolt of old garlic and cumin from the woman next door, a professor of medicine in the city somewhere, originally from Kashmir.

Ours is a neighborhood of the embattled, those who have exited borderlands, and I have only recently begun to think of what we share. We too are refugees from one kind of commu-nity that used to live all through this part of Foxboro. I used to own a construction business specializing in remodeling, but as the neighborhoods filled with different, larger families, our business oddly declined with the lack of demand. My son need-ed a home for himself and Clara after his wife left him, and I was on the verge of having to sell ours. Thus we came to our current arrangement. He works in a lumber yard, and couldn't live here if it were not for me; I could not have held on to this home with-out his income.

We are the last working-class family on our street; the others are desk jockeys and engineers, or teach at one of the universi-ties in the city, or are wealthy retirees returning to Boston. We are, or were, actually one of the few original families that have stayed in the neighborhood since before the others came from all over—Filipinos and Indians, Japanese and Chinese, Viet-namese, a few Africans. They are a reminder to me, for better or worse, of what has changed, of what our wars have brought to our home fronts, how our wars have expanded what we know. It's small comfort. Most of the area is this way, diverse in recognition of the growing international community that has arisen, and the neighborhoods are showing the strange transcendence of internationalism.

The houses are just a bit off the norm for older suburban homes. One might harbor a Ginesh near a door; another has gardens and bamboo that have taken over the side yard next to a Cape, or unusual drapes completely covering what would normally be an open picture window. Each December, ours is the only home on the street with a Christmas tree, when fifty— or even twenty—years ago, every house would have glowed in perfected holiday symmetry, and all the picture windows would have been open, inviting passersby who walked dogs or strollers to look in at the warm inventory of possessions. I walked the dog last night, and it was tough to even find a porch light lit, here where people now think in different ways of what these homes mean, and what these families might be, and the only common denominator is that many of them, in recent weeks, have decided to fly an American flag off the porch.

Most of the cars on the street are small imports, or expensive German sedans, and with each one that passes, I wonder: when will they come for his things? When will they start asking questions?

Two weeks after the accident, Nguyen Van Thieu knocked on our door. We were eating, and I could see my son considering whether to answer. His estranged wife, who turned up more and more infrequently to help with Clara, sat across the table but wasn't looking at him. She had only the occasional sad smile for me, one I felt awkward returning. My son glanced at the silent people around the table, and rose, food still in his mouth.

He opened the door to Nguyen Van Thieu stooped on the front step, sliding a manila envelope under the mat.

Nguyen Van Thieu looked up, glanced in the door to us at the table and then, clearly surprised and a little frightened, frowned before he stood. My daughter-in-law grunted, placed her dishes on the counter, and exited the kitchen, leaving Clara and me to regard one another and then return our attention to the door. Nguyen Van Thieu's frown was strained; he put a hand to his back as he stood, held out the envelope, and nodded. When my son opened the door to step out, Nguyen Van Thieu took a step back, and then put another foot down on the stoop of the porch.

My son took the envelope.

Nguyen Van Thieu said "I hope this helps." He said it with no discernible accent. I heard it in my head for days afterward, until I began to wonder whether he had rehearsed the phrase so as not to bungle it.

I was not surprised to learn that the envelope contained a wad of money. What else would one in his position put in such an envelope? But along with the money were several cards covered in handwritten script, with all the diacritical characters I recognized as Vietnamese. In the bottom of the envelope was a toy car, rusty in spots, with some dirt around it. The note attached said it was Clara's, that he had found it in his yard, near the trees, and thought she would like it back. He did not know that she couldn't play with the car. He did not know that she was strapped into her chair because she couldn't balance, or that she ate with her hand shaking food off her fork, or that she was relearning the movements she thought she knew. His note suggested we place the cards near her room for luck.

All I wanted to do was fling the car back into his yard, to

chainsaw the hemlocks, to throw nails in his snow blower, to blow up his mailbox.

Several days before this encounter, the day Clara returned from the hospital, it was as cold as we'd ever felt. She still wore a few bandages on her head and face, and could only walk while gripping her father's arm.

Nguyen Van Thieu, wearing his parka, was salting his driveway, working only a few feet from our car. Clara stepped and shifted her body to wave at him. He lifted a hand in return, but it was as though his arm had jerked reflexively, and he only realized what he was doing when the arm was halfway raised. His fingers stretched once beyond the parka sleeve then and retracted. His gaze just rested on Clara, like a thrush on the tip of a hemlock branch.

I wished she hadn't waved at all. Clara sensed something in his response was insincere, but at her age the idea of sincerity was still so new that her trouble took an abstract shape, slowing her for a moment as she turned, and then vanishing from her concern as, with great concentration, she worked toward the house. But in slipping off her, it stuck to me, and I nearly cursed at Nguyen Van Thieu.

When I asked my son what he planned to do with the money, which expenses we could cover with it, he looked at me silently. He did not, I could tell, want to use the money. I had to remind him we had little choice. I told him there are some bargains you have to make with yourself. He said this was not something to negotiate. I said the hell it was, cash is cash, and we need it. That girl needs it. He told me not to remind him what the girl needs. We never spoke of it again, but he knows what's important. When he leaves her room every night, and pauses in the dim light coming from my room, I can hear the wreck of his shoulders force its way through the night's pockets of quiet.

Because Nguyen Van Thieu has reminded me, I can hear him the way I heard everything once—the way I could sleep with my eyes open and hear the interruption of trickling water, the way I could hear the slightest breathing of earth and know when it changed to the breathing of a man. I knew this feeling, what it means to sleep on guard, with frustration, with rage at something you can hardly affect. I knew its textures despite the change in particulars and the passage of decades, despite years spent trying to unknow, or at least relearn: this powerlessness, this being pregnant with violence, this urge. I wanted to do something, but could not, and I wished for horrible things to happen to Nguyen Van Thieu for having reminded me of all of it. And more, I wanted him to suffer.

Our unit, SeaBees, built bridges and camps. The worst time was south of Da Nang, the month we built three bridges in a row, all in the same spot. The VC knew how to wait, how to sit, and we learned how to persist, knowing they watched. Or, more to the point, we knew to follow orders, not ask why: ours was to build. They would wait, they would sit in the trees with their breath of bark and mud, mold and decay, and they would watch while we sweated, put beams in place, used every scrap and bit we had, burned gas, injured men—then wait as we cleaned, broke camp, prepared departure, placed sentries at either end. When we started the jeeps to go, we'd hear a distant pop, and a second or two later, the bridge would fly to pieces.

I have never, to this day, been less than amazed by that capacity to watch and wait, and, through such patience, inflict such harm.

I have long endured fantasies of striding across the yard to strangle the widow of Nguyen Van Thieu as she sits sunbathing or weeding, but I have never seen her engaged in any such activity. I have only ever seen the car disappear slowly inside the garage, or back out just as slowly. If I see her, I do not know what I will do. She is alone and, since her husband is dead, she is a bereaved widow. Normally, that would spur me to some charity. Perhaps I would bring a covered dish, or send flowers.

The truth is, I simply want to ask her why they never told us, why it was never clear who they were. That would not change any of what happened. Or perhaps it would. Not only did they harm a little girl, but they helped to destroy an entire country. They appeared unmoved about doing either. If I see the widow of Nguyen Van Thieu, I wonder which question will come out first. Perhaps I will only express my terse condolences. But she has avoided me since I first realized she existed, so there is no reason to believe she will encounter me now.

There is another possibility: that I will do nothing and keep my distance from her. I am, after all, at a remove from the core of this. My son, on the other hand, I wonder about. He has my tendency to simmer and then to explode. He has not asked me, nor will I tell him, but this is what drove his wife away. I know because it drove away mine. There can be horror in waiting for what will eventually come out of a person you care for, fear of the pressure and the build, the brooding. Days and years of such waiting oppress. And there is no asking about it. There is no way to check. You begin to fear worse escalations, the specter of violence.

I thought I heard them argue about the money from the envelope, and I knew it would go badly, because I only heard her voice. I could imagine him though, taut, in a corner, leaning against the kitchen counter, brow oppressive and dark, his hands in his pocket, waiting for her to stop, to let him think about it. The fight ended abruptly when I heard a glass shatter. I do not know who threw it, whether one aimed it at the other, or if it was just rage announcing itself. I heard nothing afterward other than the slamming of a door.

The house simmers with absences. I listen for sounds in the heated void, remembering what I have not wanted to, thinking it over anew, from this perverse distance which, it turns out, is so close to it all. Distance mitigates anger, serving both as a means of rationalizing and of softening. But these events remind me I do not want my anger about that war diluted, nor do I want it focused on Nguyen Van Thieu.

He is only one man. Mistakes of such scale take the effort of many. MacNamara, De Gaulle, Johnson, Kennedy, Ho. More. There are, in my mind, great lines of the culpable, in legions, in some hell somewhere, waist deep in filth, fed on the corpses they made, stuffed and fed on death, their eyes pried open with bamboo talons, their gaze never shifting from the images I see now: the Mama-sans taking money for food and girls from half-starved GIs, an entire beach covered with the hosed-clean, regimented boots of the dead, and more and more, and not one image—not one—that can be uttered without its being instant-

ly familiar, a horror ground into us again and again, an abom-
ination and an absurdity for which none of the men involved
have ever accepted blame. They will never apologize. Death has
granted them release from the world which lives with their ar-
rogant mistakes.

Clara had to relearn to walk. There came a moment when the
doctors told us we would be the most help to Clara if, when
she fell, we did not immediately race to her aid. Once she figured out how to recover and could better balance on her own, it
would be best to let her struggle.

My son watched her during the summer of her recovery as
she rose, tottered, stumbled, and struggled to regain her feet.
He sat in a lawn chair, a spectator to her suffering. I heard the
din of Nguyen Van Thieu's soccer matches, somehow worming
through the hemlocks no matter how loud we had the stereo inside. The air smelled of curry from through the backyard fence.
I heard Clara's grunts, and I heard the chair creak as my son
shifted his weight. If I was in the kitchen, I would occasionally
catch her looking to her father as she worked particularly hard
to regain her feet. I heard the shredding of his patience as he
explained to her, time and again, about having to do it herself.
Her eyes never left him.

Most of the time he tried to encourage her, but not always.
Sometimes he couldn't look at her. He was near breaking once,
so I strode into the yard, took over the role of encouraging her,
held her attention for a few seconds of effort. She should not
have had to see her father tested in that way, and she should not
have had to bear that failure.

I wondered whether Nguyen Van Thieu's windows permitted

a view into our backyard, and if so whether he looked out of them. Did he watch that crime to which he was a party? I think I would have felt his eyes if he had. He had fled his country, so I do not know why I thought he might ever look back.

In a dream I smell the sting of decaying hemlock needles. I am lying on my back in a grove of trees at the edge of a great stretch of flat and cracked land. There are bones all about. Clara struggles to regain her feet and as she does her crutches kick away bones and skitter against the unyielding ground. When she is at last exhausted, the bones come together, align along a spine, go to her, and lift her. She is not afraid, and no longer appears exhausted. The bones lift her and save her. I explain that Vietnam brought us here, and she asks what Vietnam is. I begin to whisper to her about what Vietnam was, but all I can say are absurd declarations: Vietnam was a cauldron of antiseptic pigeons. Vietnam decided to be constipated. Vietnam was a vacuum in stark retreat. Vietnam was a collection of the unverified. Vietnam was the elbow of matricide. The more of these I say, the more she seems to understand.

I heard a different car in the drive one evening, and when I looked out the window, I saw Clara and her dad getting out of a minivan, perhaps a few years old, with bits of the price sticker still clinging to the windshield. I heard Clara in the house, and was about to turn from my examination of the van, when I saw my son come back to it. He sprayed Windex across the top of the windshield, rubbed at the residues with an old M*A*S*H t-shirt. When he got the windshield clean, he took a step back, then another, almost to the hemlocks on the other side of the yard. He regarded the van with an expression that puzzled me for a long time.

Later, Clara told us, in her halting speech and jittery gestures, how much she loved the new van, and her father and I worked hard to smile for her, to share her enthusiasm. We were all glad for a vehicle that was a bit more dependable and easier for her to get into. We did not mention how the back of it yawned with space, or how her mother might have enjoyed it. And we never spoke of how he was able to afford it.

It snows early. When I am spreading ice melt on my sidewalk at the side of the house, I finally see her. She totters onto the driveway, wearing his parka. Only her black rubber boots are visible under the coat. I can see in her shoulders that she is utterly lost. She is widowed, in a country far and foreign from graceful plains of rice paddies and undulations of fine-leaved grass. She is here among hedgerows, forced to be tidy, and among the many sounds of the rushing, human world.

I push into the hemlocks to watch her. She has a pail of de-icer in her left hand, and she is scattering it like birdseed with her right. She wears no gloves. Her hand is covered in rings and gaudily manicured. The smell of the hemlocks makes me want to sneeze, but I do not want her to know that I am watching her. I force my breath to become even and slow.

I remember his snow blower, its noise, his cursing. Today it is silent, however, a day without television noise, without the constant passage of cars, the low hum of others talking in far-away rooms. For this reason, when I imagine her falling, I can hear her bones break against the macadam. I hear the clatter and scratch as the pail lands and the de-icer pours out. I hear her whimper. I hear the accusation of my daughter-in-law, the shattering glass, and I hear the doctors, I hear the last breath of Nguyen Van Thieu, and Clara inside still sleeping. I hear my own breathing and I try again to slow it. I imagine the widow of Nguyen Van Thieu whimpering again before she begins to sob. I imagine my own stillness. I imagine the click deep within me as I decide to stand where I am and to watch her lie there.

BOURBON AND MILK

Your grandfather died in this room. In this chair, in fact, this chair that is brown, wooden. It is likely poplar. It is worn in the seat, so it now has two crescents of wood lighter than the walnut stain of the rest of the chair. I must also tell you that this chair has remained in this room—with the wood floor painted yellow in 1898 and again in 1950—this chair has been here since the foundation was built. In those days, families around here gathered and the men hefted the stones to one another, and a stone mason placed them. You should know, if you ever dry-lay stones, that you must be sure each stone rests on three points, like a solid stool.

As I said, your grandfather died in this chair of a stroke when he was 68. He did not fall out of the chair. His body remained here until the following morning, as your grandmother was away visiting relatives. When the mail carrier spotted him and saw a fly walking over his frozen eye, he knew it was a problem because he knew your grandfather's left eye was made of glass, and the fly was crawling across the right eye. He could see this from the tall windows by the front door, where we can see people knock during dinners. He also knew because in his final years, your grandfather would spend a moment speaking with the mail carrier. You should know the importance of being kind to those who provide you services. They are the ones on whom the world depends to run, and on whom you depend more and more. Your grandfather never forgot this. When the mail carrier stepped into the house, he found the scene as if your grandfather had only recently fallen.

His drink—you remember his favorite drink, bourbon and whole milk—it still sat on the table in a crystal tumbler. A skin had formed on the top. He had cut a butter pat and laid it on the edge of his dish. He loved to eat butter, loved the salt at the corners where his lips met, said it oiled his speech. He did not need oil in his speech. He could talk to anyone, as you recall. I know you recall this, but I need to say these things. I need to be clear about this, for you. You realize how important this is.

The butter was on the plate. The knife, its blade slick, a bead or two of moisture atop the butter, rested on the butter dish, also crystal. Your grandparents used crystal every day, and their good china, because your grandfather felt it was the ability to provide oneself with whatever small luxuries available that made one's life worthwhile. Next to the knife, his teeth rested in a cup of cloudy water. He had not yet put in his teeth for the day. If you would like, the coroner in town should still have a photo of this, and you can go look at it and see for yourself. It is not that I think you disbelieve me; rather, I realize how your own seeing will tell you stories I may not know are there. Whatever you do find, be sure to tell me, as I am telling you. There is so much to tell.

The week before he died, he went hunting with your Uncle Edward. You know your grandfather did not hunt, seldom strayed from downtown, from his routine of morning paper, meetings with Richard to discuss which chores were to be accomplished that day, and monitoring the phones for the inevitable calls. I must tell you how ironic it is that, in the end, he was not made to wait for death. He had spent a career waiting for death, waiting for the call, the one placed after the hysterical sobbing calls to family, the one where he could hear the hours of wear in a person's voice, the one that was almost always handled in the same way, with the same tones of business practicality that come to those with the fortitude to handle such arrangements. He would be very quiet on the phone, would make notes, would answer with the smallest sentences—not cold sentences, but nothing extra. It is not a time for extras. You should know this—when people experience death and you are there, do not speak unless it is needed. There is enough speaking, especially these days.

Even in his approach to the hearse, he was elegant, subdued. He would step across the courtyard to the house to tell my mother. He didn't like to actually come in to deliver his news. He would open the door, stand on the stoop stair, and call into the hallway. It was always very simple: "*Cheri*, I am off." If it was late afternoon, and dinner was nearly ready, my mother would serve us later, but put his meal on a plate, and set it in the oven. From this room, she could hear the hearse pull in to the funeral home's garage. It was where the second apartment is now. And she would always hear him, from this table, where she sat in the evenings when he worked.

She was not a doting woman, she just knew her role. At that

time, that was a role. There are too few roles today, you know, and this is why people are confused. But I do not want to talk about that. That is not what this is for. This is for the importance of a few things I want to tell you. She would sit here and either knit or read a book, or read *Life* magazine, which your grandfather loved. But when she heard his car, she knew it would be about a half hour before the click of the door handle, and he would be in her kitchen, so she turned the oven on to warm his plate, set out a tumbler, salt and pepper, the butter dish, a knife, fork and spoon—he insisted on them at every meal, even if he did not need all of them. The placemat looked naked without them, he thought. While she prepared, and the smell of his food warmed the kitchen, she tried to keep from thinking of what he was doing, rolling the body into the work room off of the hearse's garage, of he and Richard moving the corpse onto a table and sheeting it.

He entered the kitchen and my mother told me once how she smelled his work on him—she always called it his work, never any other euphemism, almost as both denial of what he did and respect for her own knowledge that she *was* denying it. Therefore, she never made any more complicated terms for it. She would surround him in other smells. She poured him strong coffee, timed to perk as he came into the kitchen. She would also make him a bourbon and milk. She would take the coat from his shoulders as he walked in and hang it on the coat rack near the furnace vent. She had always told us that she put coats there to dry. I know her better now. The coats always smelled of coal, of soot, of the warmth of the kitchen during winter. Her husband's coat would then take that smell, and so she hung it there. When she did laundry, she washed his clothes alone. She used Borax, scouring at the garments. She used lots of starch. She knew how to scrub love up against death. She knew how to cook it away so it never hung on him as thick as it did Richard. You should know about this power. You should know that you could work to push out anything. Strength is like that. Because of her he was happy, elegant, charming. Because of her, he was able to live frivolously once in a while. Too many of the people they know never had that privilege. And it was because of her that he was able to go hunting the week before he died.

He was not an outdoors man. This you know. But as you also know, he has always tried to be friends with the husbands. He wanted to be liked, just as he was respected by those in town whose families he had helped through their bad times. And that was quite a bit. When Edward mentioned he would be coming up here to hunt in the woods between here and New York, your grandfather asked to go with him. I remember Edward's surprise. His glasses seemed to twitch right on his nose, and he blinked several times before he smiled. His eyes worked to collect him. That's what I saw; eyes fluttering to draw the emotion back in. Your grandfather insisted that Edward advise him on proper outfitting, and within a day or two, he came home with a canvas duck jacket, a furry hat, a new Winchester rifle, and boots. He also purchased his first pair of blue jeans. The evening before the hunt he had her iron the jeans, as if they weren't stiff enough. Richard had also set up a target in the back yard for your grandfather, and he fired a few shots, but it wasn't long before he heard glass shatter and he put the gun down on the ground. He came in to the kitchen, took money from our drawer in the kitchen, put on a proper cardigan, and marched up the street to pay Mrs. Poirot for her window. I was surprised when they did not take offense. People today would take offense.

Your grandfather could smooth feathers like no one else. He had a bearing about him, a nose like a hawk, and very French even though straight. He had white hair at a very young age, and with his dark glasses—the serious glasses of an accountant, square, thick-framed and dark—he was a contrast of airs that made people listen to him. His mouth was trim, and when he spoke, he did so without any extra movements. His mouth was not noisy. People—even those who did not know him—put a trust in him. It perhaps also had to do with his clothes. He wore only the best. He was a peacock, all creased, tailored, and fine. He did not dress like a rich man, mind you. You should realize that it does not take money to cut a fine figure. Simply keep yourself clean, together, shirt buttons in line with zipper, tie to the top of your belt. Conservative colors. Your grandfather in a charcoal jacket, with his white hair, a carefully pressed shirt, and never sloppy at the neck. Never open. Crisp, finished with a tie.

As I was saying, when he went hunting, canvas duck jacket and dungarees with a crease, well, Edward began laughing when he picked your grandfather up. When they reached the woods it was still dark, and as they trudged in through the brush and leaves, your grandfather hardly spoke. I like to imagine that he adored the quiet, something quite unlike what he ever heard here, so near the mill and the factories, and that he might have stopped on occasion to see the sunrise through the trees, and not the window of his hearse. It may have occurred to him as well though that he was simply on another mission having to do with death, only this time he would be much closer. He never said. All he ever spoke about was his missteps on the trip. He only ever spoke of his missteps. He did so many things well, but he would not talk about them. Something you should remember. He had toted a thermos of coffee in the back pouch of his duck jacket, and when he and Edward stopped, he opened it and poured a cup before Edward noticed and glowered. Your grandfather knew nothing of deer and their sense of smell, and that the smell had effectively announced their presence. But he and Edward were soon up and walking again.

After several hundred yards, perhaps a quarter mile by your grandfather's estimate, they crossed over a rise and squatted just above a thicket of laurel. Despite the smell of the coffee, the noise they made, and the sun's steady rise, they soon saw a deer. Your grandfather did not want to shoot right away, given the mistakes he had made earlier. His restraint is something that has always served him well. Even though in this situation it was not as critical as in others, your grandfather's pause, I think, helped things between him and Edward that day. Edward needed deer meat to feed his family. Those days were not easy for him, not at all. Edward was a good man to do what he could to feed his family. As I was saying, they saw a deer. Edward stood slowly and shot. The bullet passed through its body just behind the foreleg. The animal fell and died instantly.

Your grandfather takes no credit for the death of the deer. He helped dress the animal in the field. Edward made him take the organs out of the carcass. When he told your grandmother about it later, she said she had suspected he was near tears. His voice came husky and he wouldn't look at her. I think of him out there, his arms steaming from the warm blood, his hair swirled to his arms by the moisture, the morning chill chased away in the moment of death, so much warmer than the way he found people. I wonder if he considered it more real than what he had yet done. I wonder if such reflection only comes later. I have had many more years to think about this. He died the next week.

Remember that. To those who have to make decisions and do things at given moments, they do not have the choice to reflect at the time.

Your grandmother had to wash his clothes twice. The hunting jacket hung in the kitchen until he died, and for weeks after that. I would walk to it and smell it sometimes in the weeks after he died, and all I would smell was coffee, the strong sharp smell of old blood, and coal. What I wanted to smell, and what I would like to give you, is the smell of bourbon and milk, of butter and talc, of cardigan after a light rain, and even the slight trace of formaldehyde. But we have no control over what lingers.

Maybe it will find you one day. When you do a good thing for the person you love, when you work your hardest to enjoy a day, to create a home, he'll find you then. I like to think you will smell him.

THE VISIONS OF EDWIN MILLER

At first, he wasn't sure how to react. But it was there, and he would later say to people that it was indescribably beautiful. While making his acceptance speech in Stockholm he even referred to the symmetry he did not expect. Still, at the precise moment he first viewed the image, held out in the unsteady hand of a graduate student, he thought only of puppets, of silhouettes, of dancers seen long ago in his service days, undulating behind sheets that rippled in the wind of the desert, the same movements Ella hid beneath their sheets and he almost muttered aloud that he was looking at the first stirring of sex, the kinetic movements of stirring blood. He later told her of the way the atoms were ringed as if they had splashed into matter, and she said it almost reminded her of the movement of the sea. To Edwin, such a comparison was meaningful, as Ella often moaned of the sea's curative powers. But at that moment, at the moment he beheld the lab film in front of him for the first time, with an audience of his two laboratory assistants and the other doctoral students crowded in the doorway, what he *did* actually say aloud was, "I would not have thought this believable, nor so quickly obtained." And then he left his office.

Outside the building, he walked around the back lot for air and thought, striding across the lawn until he stood under a water tower. "This," he said, pointing at it, "this is utterly a water tower." He stood for several moments before he marched back inside, through the halls of Osmond Building, upsetting the books of a lost undergraduate on his way back to the frosted window of his laboratory door, back into the laboratory to write it down. Somehow. What he wanted to write, what he wanted to say, related to the fact that what he saw—the smooth metal blue expanse of steel containing water—was utterly a water tower because the closer one looks, the greater its essential elements appear, such that if we can identify down to the very particles that comprise an object, then it is most truly there before us. It is not a trick of light and mirrors. It is not the what the sophists claim to be one other element of each person's unique perspective. Right down to the atoms that comprised it, this very thing was identifiable, atoms then steel shaped into what was, undoubtedly, a water tower.

Such was his thinking that morning in 1955. That day, Eisenhower postured as everyone's father, students on the GI Bill stopped talking so much to him about the gut wrenching facts of Korea, and cars were solidly cars, and Edwin Miller stood in his office in Osmond Building, before a lab book open on a blotter, twisting the pencil in his fingers (which he looked at a bit differently, even though he knew the moment was coming; this was no eureka—more an A-*ha*! of a confirmation, but nonetheless, now all things were different, one more small revolution in the years leading forward to the end of the century), and he wondered just what to write. He thought briefly of writing to Ella, as he often imagined when writing speeches, knowing he needed the right balance of erudition and clarity, explanation and dramatic force.

But even if he was clear, what was he being clear *about*? Lately, he had seen too much to make this vision incontrovertible, but that was only because he had no way to be sure of what he was seeing. But this, for this he had notes, an extensive series of steps that led to this, such that he could explain what he was seeing, even expected it, as alluded to in his journals. He even had colleagues who dutifully reported the results he had so studiously predicted. This was indeed what was supposed to happen, unlike the things he had seen during the day, refracted in the sun against his eyes, or during the evenings when the grainy low density of light left in the darkness of nothing seemed to him so much of a dream. He could trace the beginnings of this image so that, even if what he saw was part illusion—and as a projection he knew it would be—then at least it was an illusion with which he could be comfortable. It was rooted in him, even if the others were, ultimately, only other parts of his less tangible visions.

Heisenberg had pointed out that one could never be certain of the position of an electron around a nucleus because of both its size and the speed with which it moved. If the nucleus were an apple, the electrons existed in an area surrounding the nucleus as large as the earth in comparison. Hence, the need for orbitals, the likely trajectories of electrons, and the theoretical magnetism that held them in those trajectories. That uncertainty was

tolerable, even theoretically desirable, because it allowed for a
degree of precision in numbers once the uncertainty was viewed
a constant. The Heisenberg Uncertainty Principle allowed for the
deliberate procedure of atomic physics, providing its acolytes the
calculated margin of acceptable oblivion.

The first of his other visions had happened on what felt like
a Sunday amid the light that bathed him as though it spilled
from a bowl of sun. Edwin had unfolded his spectacles and
thumbed a hook over each ear, then pushed them to the crook
above his nose before he stood, in his nightshirt, and stretched
once, so hard that his calves felt taut, as though about to cramp.
He poured a tumbler of water in the kitchen, the gurgle from
the heavy pitcher reminding him of his bladder, and so once
the toilet routine was through, he stepped into the green patch
of his rear lawn, and heard the early buzz of insects warming
their wings against the sun. The dew on his toes was so cold he
thought they might grow numb, but he started to step toward
the field anyway. Once among the grasses, he began to skip, the
movement a memory older than anything he owned, and he was
surprised at his ability to move so, to dance with such lightness
among the tall wet grass blades, and as he skipped around in
a circle, moths fluttered into the air around him, stirred from
their meal of water on the ribs of grass blades, and bees left their
thistles, and the air shimmered with the immediacy of their
flight, a movement not of the air itself but of those creatures
that used it, that beat it with their wings, that stirred it to breez-
es, and Edwin was lifted. He had sworn his blood ran faster.

Later, he had also sworn to Ella that the event had indeed
happened, despite the fact that suddenly, amid all the dancing,

he was back among the papers of his office, thrown back in his chair so far that his arms, dangling at his sides, nearly reached the floor. He knew he wasn't dreaming, or so he thought. The fact is, it was the middle of a Wednesday, it was drizzling, and it was February. Students would soon squish into his lecture, sopping wet, the smell of their soaked wool coats overpowering the methane smell of his lab table and the underlying whiff of ethanol.

He had then risen to walk down to the lecture hall, noticed his feet were bare, and recalled that he had again taken his shoes off that morning, and so began to search about his office for them, near where he had been thinking earlier that morning, when the urge to be unshod struck him and he thought that the lack of constriction about his toes would be less distracting. As he slipped his feet back into the ragged loafers, he shuffled their clean soles against the floor, enjoying the slip, imagining the sea of movement between sole and floor, floor and earth, lost himself for a moment but regained his composure on the way to class.

The students had indeed reeked of damp wool, and a bit of the sea, from the older men in back with their Navy pea coats and surly morning beards. As he started class, an opening equation on a theoretical valence level of the particles he and his peers suspected to work about the atoms, he felt a splash of sea water against his face, up off the iron prow below. The air shoved at him with the force of explosions every few seconds, and behind him, the crew was screaming his name. He was too near the front, too near the water, he might fall in, and the planes were overtaking their vessel, and as they were being chased, they had given up the faint sight of shore for the first time in weeks.

Edwin whirled to fire, and found only chalk in his hands and a group of startled faces, and so he returned to the equation at hand and silently begged forgiveness, hoping his contrition showed through his shoulders.

So it was with recent memory of these visions that he perused the strip of film produced in his microscope, and felt that he was having another of those moments, that the fuzzy dance he witnessed was only so much of his imagination forcing the action of dust or electricity to cast unlikely shadows. Even though the image was precisely what he imagined it would be, he was worried that it so precisely matched as to be surely his projection. After the lab was empty, he found the film, brushed it with a lint free cloth, checked his own glasses, looked around for sources of light pollution, and gazed again at the field of rings blooming on the sheet. The movement was still there, the dervish, and he would think of the phrase tempest in a teacup, imagine the weather at that level, and feel his skin begin to spread apart.

He asked his team to keep the knowledge to themselves for a few days. Meanwhile, he returned to the lab for several nights after dinner to check on what he saw, repeating the steps he had recorded in faint and slanting penciled lines, working through the experiment again to be sure that others, the many who surely would challenge his findings, could easily retrace his steps. In the commotion of the days, Ella said little, performing her typical nervous vigils over the kitchen, the laundry, and the like. He hoped that she interpreted his silence as proof that he was mulling over something. She told him she noticed the depth of the crease between his eyebrows, how his hands trembled nearly all the time, how he muttered in his sleep. Edwin was not typically one to stir much about his work at home, despite its dominance of his waking hours. As she said, it was clear from how distracted he was, and from the other signs, that what he had learned, or that with which he struggled, was enormous.

Edwin rejected almost immediately the notion that he had seen into the work of God. God, of course, would never let someone like Edwin see the way that He chose to work. Edwin saw only a layer, enough to spur him on, enough to make atheists of less patient men. But for his work, he knew there had been notice. There were precious few other ways of explaining the visions, and he had tried: bad photographic paper that bubbled and burned at exposure, the activity of gas, an exothermic reaction between the glass and the gas. He knew all of those were chemically unlikely, even impossible, but he felt that since the image so corresponded with his expectation, it could not be reliable. He had seen too much of late.

One week after the incident in the lecture, and one day before he saw the filmed patterns of electrons, Edwin discovered he had been standing in the parking lot beside his car after scraping off the windshield. He knew he had been there for a while as the snow had gathered again over the windshield. He had been deep in the humid lull of a tropical forest, searching for the water from a bromeliad to refill his canteen and, spotting a large one in the crook of a sprawling teak tree above him, he had started to climb, and as his feet stripped against the bark, he felt bursts of energy from chemical reactions, as small as the rubber against the tree, the release of heat, and his feet had skidded through flashes of electricity, glowing like fireflies against the sudden night of the jungle, and as his feet warmed, he reached the bromeliad, tipped the leaves, and stretched his tongue into a stream of sand.

A sample of matter is attached, perched really, on the head of a stylus or pin that is then inserted into the glass orb, as though an Erlenmeyer flask had been inverted and slipped over the top. The result resembles a light bulb somewhat. Those noting the association between illumination, ideas, and this shape will grasp the metaphorical beauty of field ion microscopy. At once, the microscopist fills the globe with hydrogen atoms and electricity. The ion field is then supercharged and reacts with the valence electrons of the matter at the stylus' end. The microscopist has placed photoreactive paper around the globe earlier. As the ions in the gaseous field surrounding the matter react with the valence electron, light is transmitted to the photoreactive paper, and a negative picture of the atomic activity is created. Rather than counting angels on the head of a pin, the microscopist is able to make the imaginative leap to see the elliptical orbits of whirring electrons around the core of atoms. In this sense, perhaps the microscopist is counting the halos assembled over the angels, the blurry definition of the divine, the root of stranger powers than we can see.

The department chair was, of course, impressed. Edwin could see the sweat over his lip, even though a decent breeze was coming through the tall laboratory windows. He had known this was coming; Miller was good at drawing in the inevitable, at quickening the work that happened in Osmond Building, a force of gravity or light or energy that drew the other researchers out and into the constellation of work, the flurry of fire over the slate tops of lab tables, and knew that this would be no different. Edwin heard him talking, but noticed only the sudden and unsustainable growth of the fly on the department head's nose. It took everything Edwin had not to cry out, and he later knew that the department head saw the look on his face and quickly wrapped up the discussion, probably with the thought that Edwin had to go to the bathroom.

The chair had assured Edwin that the department would provide backing in addition to his grants so that Edwin could not only continue his activities, but enjoy a comfortable support. After leaving the meeting, Edwin considered what his new position would allow him to do, what he could get for Ella, what would calm her. He considered any number of the pharmaceutical items he could purchase, but then thought of a tidy dog, a Pekingese or a terrier, that might comfort her. Perhaps crystal, a vase or bowl of some sort, for her to stand or float blossoms, to bring the fields behind the house, the wilderness that she so loved, in to where it might sustain her, distract her from the vigilance she maintained over her perceived ills. He might simply give her more of himself, take a week to travel with her to the ocean, something they had not done since their honeymoon a decade ago. Many of his associates had received such counsel from their physicians, and indeed many had seemed better off for their exposure to sea air. In the end though, she might have reacted to any of these things with the same vacancy she had for most things, absorbing them into her many illnesses, smiling weakly at Edwin and returning to a suffering he had only recently started to see as originating in him.

He did not arrive at that conclusion on his own. Ella had pointed out to him that his obsession and his focus had deprived her of a husband while his position denied her the dual options of a family or work. When they met, she had been a math teacher, returning to her parents' home each evening where she waited for a man to come and marry her. Edwin did, after meeting her in the university's library one afternoon. He had stolen a glimpse at her reading, and noticed the way her face had built itself on bones that, he imagined, would hold their shape whatever her age. Then, he watched as her face did age, as the skin smoothed a bit more, then tightened and began to slack. Her eyes darkened and the hair drew away from her face. Her lips crimped slightly, then folded in while her chin swirled into a tight knob. After all of it, she looked nearly the same, her cheeks high, the widest part of her face, her nose still slightly off center, still somewhat large for her face, and her forehead still tall and untroubled. He was not so much taken with the face but with the certainty that he would actually have the privilege of watching it age. All he needed to do was kindly introduce himself, and let the rest happen.

Atoms are both matter and energy. As pressure and tempera-ture change, the behavior of electrons are affected. Electrons will sometimes jump to a different orbital level in response to a change in heat or pressure. Some results are crystallization, different bonding capabilities, or mass atomic behavior. What is important is that each change is manifest in an exchange of energy, either absorbed or emitted. The energy is a constant amount, depending on which electron moves and at what orbital level the move occurs. Such regular bursts of energy are called quanta, and therefore when an electron moves within the orbital levels of an atom it is known as a quantum leap. The movement of atoms then deals with energy that works both as particle and as continuous phenomenon, as magnetism and attraction are one existence of energy, and quanta are another. The two edge

*and ripple through systems, release and pulse, and create behav-
ior of light and matter, to exist tangibly and fleetingly, shadow
and substance at once.*

Ella would sing in the bathroom, her voice a sweet note of por-
celain, fragile and smooth. Her mother had listened to operas
during the entirety of Ella's young life in New York, in the years
when her father and mother exhausted themselves looking for
places to sing and ways to obtain food until her father resigned
to the work of a sandwich shop. He learned to love it there because the owner let him sing while building sandwiches, and
the customers began to come to the cramped storefront for the
sandwiches and the arias amid the damp acoustics of meat cool-
ers. In the end, he had obtained a version of his dream. Ella
often told this to Edwin as a reminder, saying that a slice of a
dream that resembles the whole is better than none. With the
visions he had, it was the disturbing slices of dreams that he was
seeing, and their resemblance to reality made him wonder more
and more whether he and Ella were suffering similar after-ef-
fects of their dreams.

Edwin loved to hear her sing as she bathed, the notes atomiz-
ing and drifting around the corners of the house, near tangible
in their tones, yet spreading like sunlight around him. He only
regretted that she would not let him watch her bathe and sing.
On a few occasions, he would need to get to the medicine cabinet, and she would let him in with a brief call, and as he opened
the door he was allowed the briefest slip of an image, skin ruddy
from the warm water, a skim of soap over the water, over her
chest, her arm a swatch of color whisking the shower curtain
closed. He could only imagine the rest. Once, at the beginning

of their marriage, he had pulled the curtain back to see her lying in the water, her nipples just over the water's surface, a tidal pool in her navel, her eyes wide and surprised, her neck bent to a grid of lines. He bent to touch her, but then the surprise wore off. "What are you *doing*?" she said, and Edwin stopped, half bent, his mouth just opening. He stuttered a few words, but she stood quickly and fumbled a towel around her. She asked him to go in to their bedroom and she would be in. She told him to make sure he turned out the light. Later, he studied what curves the meager starlight would illuminate, and he imagined what the shadows showed about the fullness of her body.

The day he finally saw the atom, he arrived home to a quiet house, the only sound that of water stirred and gurgling, and the soft tufts of Ella's voice in the air. She was taking a bath. He thought she was singing softly, but when he put his cheek to the door to listen like so many other times, he heard that she was crying. He knocked at the door twice before opening it, in time to see the curtain whisk shut. He said he was after his reading glasses and wondered if they were in the bathroom. When she did not respond, he told her that he had seen the atom finally, that the experiment had worked. She said she was happy for him. He said there was still work to be done. She said there was always work to be done. He said that yes, that was true, but that perhaps, still, they could visit the shore again soon. She sniffed loudly. He said that it would likely be within the month, and she still did not say anything. He finally said that the air is more curative in winter, unladed with the heated vapors of summer and the rot of seaweed and dead fish. He heard her move in the tub, and he waited a few more moments for her to say something and, when she didn't, he left, carefully clicking the door shut behind him. He was tempted to stay by the door to see whether the sobbing would resume, but went instead to his study, where he sat until dinner, watching the windows fill with the scintillating colors of tropical insects.

Edwin was convinced that Ella was a hypochondriac. Her doctor had once intimated as much to Edwin after a visit during which Ella had complained of a tingling in her arms that moved whenever the doctor tried to locate it. He had given her pills and told her to lie down in his examination room. He confided in Edwin that he had administered sugar pills, a placebo to see how Ella would react. She arose after half an hour and proclaimed the pain gone, and that she had had a pleasant rest. The doctor told her to lie down a bit more to be sure.

When she left, the doctor stared at Edwin, a stare he recognized from many of his colleagues, the stare one gives as response when all the evidence is before another. Edwin asked what he could do, and the doctor smiled. He told Edwin that psychologists interpret such behavior as a cry for attention. He asked Edwin what he did, to which the man answered that he was a physicist. The doctor folded one hand over the other and smiled, saying that he knew his profession, and that he might have phrased the question poorly. He asked Edwin, what do you do for your wife? How do you treat her? Edwin said I treat her quite well. She has everything she would want. The doctor asked how often Edwin was at home. Edwin confessed that it was not terribly often, that his work was demanding.

The doctor said, "Wives are demanding as well, Mr. Miller."

Edwin did not respond to the doctor's statement, mainly because he thought such things were not the province of a physician. Physicians, he had long thought, were little more than mechanics, and had no special lens that allowed them access to the world of ideas through their occupation. He paid the man what he asked, and once Ella was summoned back into the room, he watched her enter, her brow clear, each arm seeming to float at her sides, her steps almost ethereal.

Despite the admittedly dramatic change in a short time, Edwin remained doubtful that her pains and ailments were entirely imaginary. At times, she seemed clearly and genuinely pained or fatigued, so much so that he frequently worried, and felt at a loss for what to do. This was, however the first time a physician had recommended his time, rather than a perfunctory trip to the shore or some other destination. Still, he thought it best to combine both, to see what their dual effect might be.

In the car on the way home, Ella spoke about wanting to go to the ocean again, and Edwin wondered what the doctor had told her. She did not once ask what such a trip would mean to his work, something that rang in his head with each mention she made of the ocean. Eventually, as she quieted and they neared home, he thought of the ocean and the swirling currents of atoms within, the tides of electrons changing with depth, the constant bubbling of orbitals, the vast uncertainty contained in the weight of the seas.

The first model of atomic structure, the imaginative leap taken by Rutherford and Bohr, emerged from the Copernican model of the solar system. The later theories resembled these first impulses, providing a gravity in the machinations of electromagnetic fields, electrons in the hazy positions on their orbitals, distances in the idea of levels, pressure, and movement. Electron shift worked in the same way tides did; when electrons shifted to favor a partic-

ular side of the nucleus, resulting in the entire atom polarizing, the action turned a normal atom into one with a definite electro-magnetic field. Like ocean tides, the atom would correct itself with the influence of other atoms. But, the theoretical possibility exists that an atom might not correct in time, and that if a sample of matter were to undergo electron shift in every atom and all in the same direction, that the sample would destroy itself, as if all the oceans swept over the world at once, in one great purge of a slant-ing earth, one great curative sweep to wipe away our ills.

A month after the initial viewing, Edwin took Ella to the ocean. They had to drive over the mountain to the train station in Lew-istown on a wet and new day in March, the first sunny day in al-most a week of wind-blown drizzle. The ocean would be gray off the New Jersey cape, he knew, but he also knew that to Ella, it wouldn't matter by this point. Once it became clear they were going, she forgot all of her reservations about visiting the shore at this cold time of year. Edwin knew that she would see something there that he did not, she would inhale the air and, whether it actually affected her physiologically, she would think that it did. He remembered reading a recent paper about a substance the re-searcher had called dopamine, and his claim was that it connect-ed the various sections of the brain, communicating messages to itself. In this context, he attributed Ella's ability to react in such a way to differences in their chemical makeup. He considered tell-ing her this in the car on the way to the train station, but decided not to. It was not because he thought she would not understand it. He talked to her at length about his own work, and she fre-quently typed his notes into papers, as he was a very poor typist, and her grasp of the rudiments of English grammar was far better than his. As a result, her education in physics and chemistry was far more reasoned, theoretically sophisticated, and focused than that of many of his undergraduate students. No, it wasn't that her mind wouldn't handle it. It was that she would perceive his mention of such a difference as a criticism, as an implication that she was either crazy or inferior. Then she surprised him.

As they took their seats on the train that would ultimately land them in Cape May, she turned to Edwin and told him that she appreciated his humoring her. She said it as she rested a hand on his shoulder, stroking down the wool fibers in his coat. She would not look directly at him. As she spoke about how she understood that her need for the ocean may seem strange, Edwin watched as her hair began to dull, then to grow more wispy, to drift off of her scalp in great sheets that slid past her shoulders. At length, it was only her graying skull that sat next to him, and he sat as still as he could in his seat, knowing now that the moment would pass, and praying for it to do so.

By the time they reached the train station in West Cape May, Ella had slept well, Edwin had enjoyed a few gin rickies, and their cabin had filled with cigarette smoke that seemed to dampen the conversation, to pillow all of the noise of the train. As they rode in the taxi to their hotel, the dampening continued, the ocean's waves dulling all the rest of the sound, so that Ella's voice sounded more like a stage whisper than a voice, a clutter of clicking and rushes of air, and to Edwin it did not matter so much what she said, but that she was talking in such a rush, was so moved to speak with him that she hurried. Had he not seen her behavior at home, he would not have thought her sick during this display, until she finally paused and, resting back in the seat, let her face shut down, her eyes close, her body take on the look of sleep even though he knew her to be awake.

Their room overlooked a spit of rocks that left the shoreline and pushed out into the sea, away from the coastal road that also passed below his window. The shore was awash in the yellow light of gas lamps, still maintained in this small city that never seemed to age. Aside from the hotel they were in, the largest building by far within sight, the streets were a neat jumble of Victorian homes, blocks of gingerbread and clipped boxwood, the lush tail fins of the cars in the street a contrast to the minutiae that trimmed the houses. This time of the year, most of the houses were closed to guests, but he could see from his window one of the horse-drawn wagons that vacationers loved to ride in. As he stood at the window, waiting for Ella to finish her bath, he wondered if a vision would come to him then, accompanied by the vertigo that came from being several stories above the ground. He thought then that conscious thinking about them probably kept them from occurring, even though their incidence was not something upon which he preferred to reflect.

The next day, he knew, would be decisive for Ella. They would sit in rented chairs, bundled against the wind, and watch the ocean come in. Ella would inhale deeply. They would have lunch at one of the tiny restaurants that were still open, and they would eat outside if at all possible, crab cakes on brown paper in a basket, the oil spotting broken rings around the cakes. Then, they would return to their seats in the sand. It would sustain them both for a little while.

Is there the possibility of the death of an atom? Not really. It is believed that atoms can substantially change their behavior at extreme temperatures, but the conversion of matter entirely to energy is impossible. Rather, at or near absolute zero, or -273 on the Kelvin temperature scale, electrons in a gas would become so chilled that their movement would be nearly arrested. Under such conditions, the atoms would lose their separate identity character-istics and the mass would behave as a single entity, the so-called Bose-Einstein condensate, a theoretical state of matter posited by Einstein and the renowned Indian mathematician Satyendra Nath Bose. Such conditions have not yet been produced, but the theories hold up, as matter can neither be created nor destroyed, and be-cause the characteristics of molecules have been shown to exhibit the possibility for change under extreme temperatures. Physicists already know that some such modification has to exist for those phenomena writ large, such as stars. But at the smallest instances, when the characteristics of matter are so fundamentally changed, does the resulting entity gain the fleeting permanence of energy as it is released? When a body slows to such a state, what is left for it to hold?

After lunch, after they resettled into their chairs, and after Ella's deep breaths and serene closing of her eyes, after a long hour wherein the only sound they heard was surf, Ella died. At first, Edwin only noticed that she was not inhaling as lustily. Then, he noticed her repose, the most calm he had ever seen her. As he thought about her illness, its strange offices and the mystery of it, he realized then that such repose could be dark, could be a totter-ing near death, the last murmurs of a heart folding in on itself. He touched her shoulder, and when she did not snap awake as usual, he slid his hand down her arm and rested it on her hand.

How little it takes to stop a body, he thought. How much we can endure, how little it takes.

He did not wonder what he had missed. He did not stop and consider what signs might have been there. He knew much of that would come later, and so he made himself simply sit and enjoy the last of her company. When recollections of the physician came to him, he suppressed them, thought of Ella bathing, and her voice like a water chime. When he started to think of the psychologists, he instead made himself think of Ella's fascination with mathematics and her nearly forgotten passion for teaching. When he began to think of what he would have to do tomorrow, and the next day, and on into funerals and research papers, letters to friends and speeches to other physicists, he instead concentrated on trying to call one of his images, to see if he could do it, to see if he could force Ella back for the few moments of hallucination that might allow him to say something, not that he had any idea what it would be.

He knew then that he had seen the atom. It had not been a vision, it had not been a trick. Why the realization would come at that time he didn't really know; perhaps it had to do with the fact that his thoughts were intensely deliberate and intensely his own, as he groped for ways to deal with the moment at hand. In so doing, it opened channels he hadn't considered, and so realization was able to surprise him.

The ocean was making noise now, wind-pushed and violent with cold, healing and deafening. All physics pushing it along, life and the rest of it preserved in salt. He thought of beginnings, of their tidy brick house and the bed where he would sleep the following night. His dreams would be made of this, and he would force himself to remember that all visions were simple arrangements of light.

A Country of Shoes

Olena had tired of hanging the paintings weeks ago, and so Michael's daily visits had grown more and more tense. At first, she would hear his truck and grin to herself, close her reading spectacles and let them hang on the chain her husband Bodhan had purchased for her, or she would place a spoon on its rest and turn a burner down, or she would place the watering can down on the cracked bricks in the back garden. Michael's arrival once meant the advent of pleasing work, seeing the icons and pastures and noble portraits again, seeing the colors she had missed for months on end, seeing the promise on her wall of all they would bring to her and Bodhan when they were sold.

Now, her spine stiffened when she heard the burping sound of his truck idling in the driveway. Each time a corner of a frame knocked the door jamb, or when he slid a large work along the plastic liner covering the hall carpet, the skin at her neck would prickle. At first, his visits meant she would pull down two of the small, cut crystal glasses that had been her grandmother's, and she would pour each of them a glass of wine. She hadn't poured him a glass in weeks. Before, he had stood in the kitchen, the way bellmen stood inside rooms in American hotels, with that look that she took almost as a scolding. But he was neither as stupid or persistent as a bellhop. He stopped eventually.

She had even grown more cross with Bodhan. During the days, she kept quiet. He drove at night, drove taxis, drove students to bars and back. It was less dangerous than the marshrutka had been, less dangerous than his trips to the ports in Odessa, especially in the years just after the Soviets reluctantly gave them back their city and the Russians came in only to try to buy everything not nailed down. The new job had far less dignity. He came home frustrated.

The other day, he had slumped at the kitchen table as usual, pulled out his box of Belos, and she told him, "Don't smoke."

She pointed to the paintings.

"That's crap," he said—another charming word he'd picked up from his fares.

But she knew otherwise. She had not realized how yellow their rooms had been in Odessa until she first walked through the fourteen white rooms of what would become her new home. Each room had been newly painted, and the realtor had told them this with a smile bright as a new car. The carpet was new, and while it was not white, the shade of brown might as well have been white, all one tone, all blending into the walls in the corners where the shadows met. She felt, at one point, that even the new asphalt driveway was white, as it was so clear of seams, blemishes, rises, or anything that might reveal the fact that it was made by imperfect men.

Bodhan was the king of imperfect men. He had always been a

loiterer in their home, holding court at the table of their apartment when the unemployed men would sniff out their open door and the sharp smell of his horrible Russian tobacco and would come and sit with Bodhan and drink and beg cigarettes and put up with his opinions on art and the tides and shipping and opera, his condemnation of the Buddhists who lived below them in their silent and efficient way, or of the politics, newly emboldened by the fact that Odessa's political threats were no longer specific, no longer particular, and therefore, in their vagueness, almost silly. None of the other men said much, getting quietly drunk while her husband's fog of invective and brittle wit hung over them all. But now, he sat and, without an audience, drank quietly, made notes in the little book he'd taken to carrying in the breast pocket of his icily translucent blue shirts, picked his toes. Olena once caught him digging lint from under the nail of his big toe with a silver butter knife.

"It is not crap," Olena said. "Michael has worked very hard—"

"He has worked very hard to do something no one asked him to do," Bodhan thundered.

Michael had written her first, detailed how many he had been able to save, how many he had gotten out of her Moldavanka gallery, then out of the apartment, how he had covered them and driven them around, using the network of drivers to get them out of the city, out of the region, and then out of the country. He had rented an apartment in Zagreb, elaborately expensive because it had climate control, and he stacked the works there. He arranged for their passage out on a freighter run by a Pakistani captain cagey enough about searches to be able to hide things in plain sight.

And he had done all this without Olena voicing any kind of

request, without—as far as she could remember—even affecting the posture of any entreaty. But Michael also never asked why Bodhan and Olena left without him, why they left by night, why he had to work hard to find them once he had arrived in France and, later, Portugal, before sailing for America. Through all of it, he was not exactly selfless. Their arrangement over the years implied that he would have much to gain if they were able to move the works in America, but it was also a risk, as Americans tended to want to know everything, get all their questions answered. Michael knew it—had even once said as much, wearing as much disdain as he could, during a meal with Olena and Bodhan, so much so that Olena thought the disdain cultivated specifically to impress Bodhan, though she did not understand why. Bodhan had never uttered a single kind word about her half-brother, other than to imply that it was not entirely his fault he was damaged, since his father was "profligate"—another fine instance of Bodhan trying on one of the more interesting new words he'd picked up.

But Michael persisted. There was money to be made, and Olena agreed. And there were many pieces among the collection to get rid of, property that had remained a risk to them for long enough. And with the perfect hiding place—a prefab in a patchwork neighborhood next to a college campus, where art amid bohemian shabbiness made perfect sense—they would be crazy not to make a final push.

So when Olena heard the truck again, earlier than usual, the door slam and Michael's cheery whistle, she stood at the edge of her bed, shushed the man in it, who smelled nothing of cigarettes and wool, and instead of meat, the air outside, chemical mint and citrus, an engine—all things vaguely American to her—and said she would not be long, but that *these are things I have to be done with.*

Michael came to the door as she arrived herself to open it, holding her robe in her fist at the front of her. Underneath the robe, she was sweaty, still wet, her hair a mess, her skin tingling with what she remembered and wanted to return to. She wondered what about her condition showed through the robe as Michael shouldered the door, ridiculous tanker-sized white tennis shoes clumping on the stoop, and shuffled through it a Byzantine frame covered in packing paper.

"There are two more," he said.

She put a hand to her lip. Cool air bathed her toes as it rolled in the front door. A toilet flushed, and though she heard it, the sound was faint. *What was he up to, what was he thinking?*

"I saw your husband," Michael said, returning down the entry hall.

She raised an eyebrow—*And?*

"How many more do you have today?" she said.

He stood in the doorway, glanced at the truck, and then back at her. His eyes lingered on her chest, then her hip, before he said, "I said it now: I have two," He met her gaze. "Will you help me?"

"I'm not dressed," she said. "Which ones are they?"

"One of them you like," he said, grinning, still looking at her body. "The little boy holding the cat."

His hair, the color of fresh cream, something she had not seen since she was a girl, combed on to the canvas, as if the artist had layered strokes to equal the number of hairs on the head of his model. The warm shirt, a boundless red. Everything about the piece was lavish, someone who knew he had time and food had painted the work slowly.

"Will you help me?" he said again.

"Bring them in so I can hang them. You can come back then and have tea and we can look at them."

"Tea is not something I do now," he said.

"Well, then just bring them in. The morning is cold, Mykhail."

He glared for a moment. Ever since he had been in the U.S., he had insisted on Michael. And drinking coffee. And wearing enormous shoes. Olena found it tiresome but useful to remind him on occasion of his new pretentiousness.

He shrugged. She would not help him. By the time she dressed, he'd be done, and she was not like one of those women in her neighborhood who worked in their yard or walked their ridiculous pets and wore sweatpants or pajamas or whatever.

He accepted the answer. "Are you buying a new car? Without letting me know?"

"No," she said.

"Well, I saw Bodhan looking at a car. Something big, four doors. Like a low-hanging truck."

"I don't know why he would be doing that," she said. "But so he is not telling me about it—so what?"

He kept talking, telling her to make sure Bodhan didn't do anything stupid, and she pointed out the difficulty in getting things like tides and the pull of gravity to change, much less something difficult like Bodhan. But Michael kept going, one admonition after the other, as the chill of the morning crept into her, and the bedroom she had left likely grew lighter and colder itself. When he started talking about people he knew who had expressed interest, about moving some of the icons, she wanted to listen more carefully, but felt then the serenity of knowing the money would come, the confidence in the trusting nature of their new country and its wide-eyed citizens, and the ease with which people who bought art would listen to an accent from someplace they would never understand.

"You worry too much," she said at once. She must have interrupted him when she did, because he looked it.

"Don't let him buy the car—at least not while this house is full," he said. "Make him wait."

Bodhan, stupid, smelly, weak, stumbling Bodhan. "He has waited long enough," she said. "Let him buy a car." *And, she thought, let me go back. There is a man in my room wanting fucking. Let me go back.*

She told her lover, the art professor, a story he, too, would know. The young man was unattached, from Greece, and he took pictures of his house every week to mail to his father to show him that it was real—*see how the trees grow, Papa?* he would write, *see how it looks a little different each time, how I have painted the window trim and put up a fence? Do you see?* She told him a story she had heard herself, from her countrymen, from others in the town, the story about the moment in the grocery store. *All of us have it*, she said. The one where you go to the grocery store, usually right away, once you hit the country, taken by some friend who himself had been taken by another, a hand to the elbow, to show them. And at the sight of the variety, of the abundance, of the disregard that Americans had to what surrounded them, men wept, women laughed, children gorged themselves.

But for me, Olena said, *for me it was different.* She had known what to expect, had heard all about it. She was unmoved in the produce section, and although the aisles, too, surprised her with just how much could be had, it did not unseat her. But when they went to check out with the makings of a meal, she saw in the checkout aisle two tins of shoe polish, one black, one brown. And then a kit that contained both colors—and it hit her that people owned many pairs of shoes, and she remembered her own brother—not Michael, her father's bastard and her half-brother, but the other one, the *real* one, who died in Afghanistan, the soldier, who had one pair of shoes forever. One summer he grew so fast that the shoes no longer fit and her father cut out the toes because his feet had grown faster than the soles had worn. Her brother had died only ever owning a single pair and now she lived in a country of shoes.

Her professor had shoes—teaching shoes, walking shoes, going-out shoes, and different kinds of running shoes. The running shoes had taken him past her home each morning, and he had noticed in the weeks since she and Bodhan had moved into the house that the front room had steadily filled with columns of paintings in carved frames, icons embroidered or painted on dingy fabric, and shelves sporting saints painted on boards with gold leaf flashing like sequins as he ran past. The paintings drew him the most, covering the walls, sometimes four or five in a single column until they reached the ceiling. He had noticed, too, he told her, that the only furnishings to go in the room were straight-back chairs and a very old davenport the color of strong tea and with a back curved like a woman reclining on her side. The first time in her bed, he told her that he couldn't stop thinking about the house because it had a room like a museum, where the people who lived there thought enough to put seats—and only seats—in the room, to look at the artworks without the distraction of anything else. Olena climbed onto him then, thrust herself over him, and stopped his mouth with hers.

The chairs were Bodhan's insistence. *People will be wanting to look at them, and we as hosts must seat them.* She had wanted the artwork spread through the house, inconspicuous, hanging such that their abundance was at least not concentrated. *This is America,* Bodhan had said, *no one will notice a lot of anything.* Fitting that she was fucking the one who noticed.

For months, the works came cheap, or easy, often both. Bodhan would meet people on the street near train stations, frames standing off behind them in an alley or in a car parked nearby, and they would be selling them for anything but rubles. If he had a half liter of vodka or whisky on him, that could get him a painting. The remainder of a sandwich Olena had made, or an extra shirt in his cab, or a watch someone had given him for a long last ride out of the city while weeping in the back seat—anything could fetch a treasure long held in a family.

Then men with dollars started appearing near the train stations, near the hovels left that could pass for hotels, near the brothels, and they knew enough to be patient, to offer something not quite top dollar but that offered a transferable power in any city to which someone would be running. Once, when Bodhan had bought a painting from a man with liquor and a free ride—and effectively swiped the buy out from under the nose of one of these men who seemed always dressed in heavy black suits with shoulders like mountains—he parked for lunch only to return to his marshrutka to find a washing machine sitting smashed into its windshield. He walked around the car in

silence, the street around him, too, quiet, despite the people everywhere in doorways smoking, and he heard a flute playing,
and someone sobbing, and the wings of pigeons suddenly beating the air as they rose at the sound of an ambulance roaring
through an intersection. As it passed, Bodhan looked up to see
it was missing both its driver-side and passenger doors. When it
was gone, no sounds remained on the street, and the building's
ashen bricks grew more pale as the sun came out from behind
a cloud.

He bought a new cab, and for weeks and then months people
talked to him as he drove it—when they spoke at all—of what
would happen to the country, the city, their street, but never in
questions. His fares made declarations. The Soviet Union was
gone but also still everywhere. Everything now was for sale. He
heard of fires in Moscow, fighting in Donetsk, people stepping
over bodies left in the street in Leningrad, and he soon heard
tell that the drive to Moscow, long and perilous though it may
be, was often worth it for spending a weekend acquiring all you
could stuff in your car. Each week, a new parlor caved in, the
front was torn off a home, a museum was suddenly open to the
weather and to plunder. With the Soviets hungry and wandering
in their uniforms of dust, the police looking only for food, the
once hidden treasures of the cities east of the Urals and down to
the Crimean gurgled to the surface of the heaving country like
a kind of oil.

Twice Olena accompanied him on trips, one to Moscow, one to
Stalingrad, and each time she marveled at how he became a different man. He still smoked, but did so slowly, waiting for a long
time between pulls, his lips taut. He spoke little—gone were the
opinions. Or, at least, quiet they were. His bootlickers not there

to receive whatever he deigned to drop. But he was not withdrawn. He would make an observation now and again, or would answer something Olena would say with a lengthy story. Even with their car full on the return trips, woolen blankets covering the mess of plunder stacked in the cramped bench of the back of their Volga, he drove as if they were on some errand, as if retrieving a part for a factory that their comrades expected would take a week to fetch. Only once on either trip did he display temper, when a large portrait of an officer distantly connected to Nicholas II did not fit, and he chipped the carved wood frame, cursing that he should have brought his marshrutka.

She thought of that man now, the pensive storyteller, the relaxed pilot of that car working its way past dead cows and long, charred fields, over bridges shaking with disrepair, with all the concern of—she loved this phrase—*a Sunday driver.* He had been at rest, Bodhan perhaps purely himself.

Now, her professor sat in one of the chairs in their living room—the room she would always refer to as the parlor, a ridiculous name in this informal place—and drank tea while looking at the walls.

"These all—these were in your family?" He seemed ready to laugh and she did not know why.

She shrugged. "It's a big family."

He stared at them again and then stood. "You're not even pretending to tell me the truth," he said. His smile spread.

"I am not being honest about too much, am I?" she said, and reached for his crotch.

He hopped back and set his tea down. "Really," he said, suppressing a laugh. He worked at stilling his face. "I mean, how did you come by all this?"

"Does it matter?" she said. She was still in her bathrobe, and she felt the sun through its sheer fabric, thought about how his neck would smell something like the sea, something like whatever home was left somewhere far away.

He crossed his arms. "Huh," he said. He pointed to the painting of the boy with the cream-colored hair. "Who's this? What's the story here?"

Why did he notice these things? Why could he see so easily, and what made him pick *that* one, what drew his finger to point to a head dearer than anything she would ever see again? A horse kick, a fence post, burlap against the blood, matting into his hair, the long muddy road down to something resembling a town, the jostling ride to a doctor, and all of it nothing, nothing more than rain or swirling sun or a day that went on in spite of the end of one kind of world.

"It doesn't matter," she said, and was surprised at how much deeper her voice had become. When she crossed her arms, she rubbed at the roughness of her elbow through her thin sleeve.

"I'm beginning to think it does matter," he said. "I think it matters a lot."

"People here—you think everything has some huge meaning. Everything is so important."

"Well, things matter. Your past, your family, your country—"

Shaking her head, she said, "Take me to bed. Just take me back to bed."

He thought about it; she could see that plainly. She stood as still as she could while she waited for him to make up his mind. The concentration made her weary.

In bed, he told her to leave the reading glasses around her neck, to let them dangle on the chain. It caught the morning light and scattered it across her body, and the professor watched, and she felt the glasses knock against her chest.

Michael brought sandwiches wrapped in butcher paper and taped, their prices written in grease pencil right on the wrapper. They were as large as the head of a goat, and too much. He devoured his like it was his new bad habit. Olena picked at hers, waiting for him to get to his news, the news that prompted the phone call, the shout of a pending visit, the phone call that, after so many days, should at least have been from the professor. Something.

Michael finished chewing and told her of his buyer, a private collector, an expat who had relocated to Pittsburgh, who owned apartments in town, as well as in Johnstown, Greensburg, Pittsburgh, all near colleges. They were palaces, he pointed out, but the students still were a never-ending river of complaint. Olena wondered if the clumsy reach of language was Michael's or if this apartment man had said it. The catch, of course, was that they had to meet the man in Pittsburgh, had to bring the works to him.

"Of course. That is not a problem," she said.

"It is a huge risk," he said. He chewed thickly, bovine, his teeth side to side. "Taking everything is not a good idea. It's a three-hour drive through mountains. We could crash, get pulled over, we could make many of the mistake."

She waved at him. "We don't need to take many. How many could he be interested in? Truly?"

Michael went on—this collector was an important man, a fierce man, someone who helped fund Yushchenko's campaign for election as Ukraine's president, and even helped with the medical treatment after the saboteurs had tried to poison him. He was a man of taste—wine cellar, many cars, horses, different homes. He had been a strong man once, in Izmail, working for hotels, moving women from place to place, before he fled to Lodz, and then to the United States in the early 60s. Michael tried on another phrase: "He is a man not to be trifled with."

She laughed. "Do you know what that means?"

He chewed. "I know enough."

"Tell your collector we will bring him some things to consider. Set it up."

Michael did not speak until he had consumed his sandwich and folded the paper to slip it back into the empty brown bag. "I will need money."

Never does a man come into this house, she thought, *that does not want something from me.* He was staring at her again, at her chest, like a dog. He rubbed the top of his thighs. Like a child, he sat. She let him. When she stood, she did so slowly, bending first, knowing how the scoop of her blouse would dip, knowing that in moving slowly Michael would keep quiet, divided, both aroused and sickened in formless but paralyzing ways, and she let him twist with it before standing.

"Wait here," she said.

In the bedroom, she nearly slipped when she stepped on the shimmery pool of her robe on the floor. The coverlet lay near it, the bed stripped of its sheets down to the mattress, the laundering overdue, too fragrant with the professor to go any longer without washing. His scent had almost overtaken Bodhan's earthen huff, though her husband himself could smell nothing with his nostrils long charred by first Soviet and then horrible Russian tobacco. Behind the dresser, from a fire safe pushed

A COUNTRY OF SHOES

into a former fireplace, she pulled a manila envelope and drew out cash, a fist of fifty-dollar bills. Counting it in the room, she heard Michael cough, heard paper crumple, then his comical footsteps in his grotesque shoes as he wandered through the kitchen.

She counted the money slowly, feeling the grit of the bills, taking in their metallic smell, the smell of the envelope itself, and felt the sudden tug at her throat as if she were about to weep.

With any luck, the collector would buy it all, and perhaps burn it all, or hide it deep in one of his many houses, or dig a hole and hide it all from the sun.

When she handed the money to him, Michael said, "This is probably too much."

"Take every precaution," she said. "Make the deal work. Do what you have to do."

"Does Bodhan—"

"In this, Bodhan does not matter." As she said it, she shuddered. If Michael noticed, he was not saying anything.

Olena felt the roar before she heard it, through the wall of her bedroom, and she realized it was in her driveway, before the garage, and her first thought was to wonder if whatever it was would burst through the wall and crash over the paintings stowed there still, snapping frames and cedar boards, lacquer flaked and chipped, dust kicked up.

Then she heard her name barked. Bodhan.

She shoved her book under the mattress, slipped her phone into her pocket, and strode out to the front room. In the street, directly in front of the expansive window of their parlor, rumbled a car as long and dark as a hearse, its grill like straightened concertina wire or mesh black baleen, its tires deep in the wells like spies. It was a car the KGB might have driven, and here Bodhan was, sunk shoulder-deep in its cabin, in a seat probably softer than he had ever known in a car, with room for seven fares. His face was joy. His face was America. His face was smiling like it hurt, as if a dream had elbowed its way to the surface and he was pleased to have the pain. His cruelties, his bombast, his pinched view of the world, his *crap*—they shrank before him. As if his face was that of a godly clown, the weary and tired and beaten cowered before it. She didn't know whether to laugh at the image she created or to step out and wave at him. He could see her, and she knew he waited for something, and so she stepped out the door and waved.

"What are you thinking, you stupid man?" she said to herself.

His smile fluttered, a leaf in a sudden breeze, and he turned from her. He looked down once to the dashboard, then lifted his chin, sat back, and the car floated away from the front of the house. He drove it like an exhibition. Polished bright as a shoe, it glided away into the neighborhood, slower than the bikes ridden by students and professors returning from classes, slower than the leaves drifting in the light breeze, slower than the reflections of trees and windows and mailboxes and shrubbery and garbage cans that poured across the black fenders gleaming like the shoulders of an onyx icon.

The car moved slow like an omen, like a storm striding across a field to a paddock bathed in sun, to a black horse lathered from a long and punishing run, slow like the arc of a hoof, or the seep of everything good into a dusty ground. The car gleamed like blood, black like a void. She was shaking as she watched him, both hands gripping a wheel—she had never seen him look so horrified, so unnatural behind a wheel. The thing was larger than anything either of them had known.

Tell me about the boy, the professor said. Though she met him at the door wearing only her robe, sash undone, leaving it parted, though she met him and let the morning air wash over her body until it tingled, and let her hand run in tripping flits down his sweaty chest, though she yearned to lap the salt from beneath his chin, he stayed dressed, walked past her and into the gallery room, stood by the chairs and the tea-colored couch and fixed his gaze on the boy. *Tell me about him. It is a different work than the rest. Newer. Someone you know did this?*

She stared at a crude rendering of the Christ laying across his mother's lap. Dying, bloodless, more about light and sorrow than the grit of death. The boy's head had lain in dirt, and they had never managed to wash it all out afterward. He had already gone to the earth. Bodhan had lacked the pull to find a priest. The boy had gone into unconsecrated ground. They lived thousands of miles from his bones.

"There's nothing to say," she said. She did not care whether or not he believed her.

He sat looking at the wall, staring at the boy. She peeled off her shirt, said, "I want you to fuck me now," and pulled him from the room.

"How can you—" he started.

"Because it does not matter," she said. "Everything is crap."

Bodhan wore his favorite jacket, one Olena had long despised— it smelt of old smoke sifted and worn into the loosening wool weave. The sleeves ended well above his wrists, so his shirt cuffs flared around his hands. He had put on an expensive watch, and it chuffed softly against the padded steering wheel of the new car every time he took a turn.

He was a different man beside her. The car moved as if on air, and he drove it with will—not with the casual control he had shown in the marshrutka, not with the delicate fear he had shown in the road before their house. He drove it as though he were taking a test—not a terribly challenging test, but one to which he had to pay some attention.

They had packed half of what they had acquired into the car, far more than Olena thought possible. Michael had helped, layering sheets between individual pieces, arranging the trunk to fit dozens of works, stacking many others in the back seat. At first, he had insisted on accompanying them, but Bodhan pronounced that him sitting in the car where paintings should go could cost them potential sales. When Michael retorted that he would watch the house, the skin at the nape of Olena's neck prickled. She had not told the professor she was leaving, and could only imagine what would have happened had he shown up.

"The house is fine," she said. "It's a good neighborhood. No one is poor. No one wants anything. We could leave the lights on, door open, money on the table and it would be there when we got back."

Michael shook his head, his expression all but growling *stupid woman*, but Bodhan said, "She is right. Stay away from the house. Too much goes in and then out there anyway."

Olena thought both men entirely too paranoid about things that simply did not matter in this country, but held herself in check. Michael would not be blundering through their house, meaning that for her, all was well. Even once they were riding, even as dark fell and Bodhan leaned forward, as if waiting for the headlights to fail, even as she worried about how unkempt he looked, how much he stank, what new word he would try out on the collector, she felt wonderfully at ease. She was alive in a country that did not follow you, where order was an agreed-upon condition, and where precious little mattered to anyone, making the wide road ahead of them something sublime as a sea or the sky above incomprehensible mountains.

It helped that they were also about to unload the cursed paintings and icons, to a man who, if Michael was to be believed, would pay enough that she and Bodhan could do whatever they wanted. She thought of the professor then, wondered what he would do, what she would do, once Bodhan was at home, no longer driving. *That will be fine*, she thought. *It doesn't matter.*

The conversation was easier, and the collector, while strong, thick in the arms and neck, wore clothes fit as though made just for him. As she had the thought, Olena thought of her father, who grew up a tailor's son and had intended to be one before he was pressed into a factory, and then figured that the clothes probably *were* made just for this man. Bodhan spoke in a measured way, without haste or invective, and the man nodded, such that the exchange and the wine and the mussels and the brioche and the foie gras all combined to nearly have her asleep. She had a flash of worry—*this man is making us soft, he is feeding us too much*—and looked to the napkin in her lap as nausea swelled in her, and then she saw his shoes. Tassel loafers, polished and clean, but simply cut. The tassels were the closest thing to an ornament, and even then, considering they were a perfunctory component of such a shoe, they were hardly an excessive ornament. They were barely an ornament at all.

She wanted to ask him how many pairs he owned. The sides were worn, and the leather lightly marked, but someone had taken pains to clean and buff them, to make them last. If he had a nicer pair, she reasoned, he would have worn them. When she looked up at him, he was listening to Bodhan discuss their neighborhood, his face open as a church, as if Bodhan were telling a story about the man's mother, and how many admirers she once had. He looked as happy as a boy. *He may own enough houses to make a village,* she thought, *but he is at heart a simple man.*

He told Bodhan he would take probably everything in their car. They drove behind him to his home, a sprawling brick palace in Fox Chapel that nonetheless had small windows and expansive wood trim. He took off his jacket, rolled his sleeves, and he and Bodhan unloaded the car, stacking the works in a kitchen cleaner and larger than any Olena had ever seen. Afterward, he poured them sherry, gave them cash, and they toasted Ukraine several times.

Once they were again on the road, it was miles before they exchanged words of any kind. They simply laughed, hard enough that Olena ached and wept and clawed for Bodhan's hand to grip in her own.

Where the door had been forced, the wood splintered and the jam hung away from the building. The chairs in the front room had been moved back, lined up against the window, next to the couch, and the wall, bright and empty, held a few nails still left in the plaster. Most of the nails were now on the wood floor.

Bodhan roared and fled the room, off to the rest of the house, to the kitchen and bedroom. His feet thundered over the floors as Olena stood in the front room and took in all that remained—crystal glasses in a cabinet, the television they bought and seldom watched, the computer Bodhan never let her use. She walked to the bedroom and knew in an instant that Bodhan had not made it there yet.

She bent to her pillow and gathered the yellow-haired boy to her chest. Then, as quickly as she could, she wrapped it in a nightshirt and pushed the frame into the closet.

"They took them all!" Bodhan hollered. "All of them!"

She almost yelled back, "It doesn't matter," but the words caught in her throat.

THE MECHANICS OF HEAT

Midway into the second quarter, the little punk from the 79-year-old youth soccer carwash team finally connects with Kayla, his blunted cleats grazing her shin, the shin guard popping out of her sock as she tumbles into the mud.

"That little shit," Maury says, and then he is on his feet, screaming to the referee, some hung over frat boy college kid out in the bright Saturday sun. The kid turns his head just slightly toward Maury before blowing his whistle, and as the kids stop and their heads spin looking for the violation, Maury runs onto the field.

Kayla stands and brushes at the dirt ground into the front of her jersey. "It's stuck in the holes," she says to her dad.

"It's okay, Kayla, are you hurt? How do you feel?" Maury kneels and looks at her face.

She pokes her fingers at the mesh of the jersey, clawing at the dirt trapped in it. Maury sees her shin guard laying a few feet away. "How is your leg?" he asks.

"Okay," she says, looking down, and her lower lip pops out

after she says it. Her voice is small, as if she detects his urgency and is responding to it.

"Wait here," he says, and he strides to the shin pad.

The frat boy ref calls to him. "She alright?"

Maury says, "Yeah, no thanks to you. You should pay attention, throw that kid out of the game." Somewhere behind him, Maury hears a parent concur.

"Hey man, it's a game, and she's okay," Frat Ref says. "Things like that happen."

Maury tries to grin, to hold back. "Don't have kids, do you?"

"What's that got to do with it?"

Maury looks at him, at his neck flecked with ingrown hairs. "I hope we're not paying you much."

Frat Ref is about to say something, but Maury sees the boy's eyes shift to something behind him, and when he turns, he sees a short man with a pinched face approaching. He wears an enormous fur hat, wholly out of place in the morning, in April, on a soccer field in Port Matilda. Maury stands.

When the other man speaks, his accent is heavy, Slavic. "Do you try to have my kid thrown out of the game?"

"Was your kid the one that checked my daughter?" Maury says.

"It is a game. That is what you do, they do. Kick, run, score," the man says.

"Kick run score, yeah, not fucking kick one another."

"Sir, can you bring the language down a notch?" Frat Ref says.

"I am not saying well," the man continues. "You know how the game is, kicking."

"What? What the fuck are you trying to say?"

"Sir," Frat Ref persists.

"Shut up, John Boy," Maury says, then returns his attention to the Slavic man. "Spit it out, tell me your problem."

"Sir, you're really letting this get out of hand."

"I am? *I* am? We wouldn't be here if you'd use that whistle once in a while," Maury says. He realizes he's nearly screaming. "These kids, you gotta watch them, they can get hurt."

"Perhaps your girl is not handling it," the other man says. "You take her out of the game. My boy is good. He plays good."

Maury spins. "Your kid's a fucking menace."

"Dude, I'm gonna tell you to go home in about three seconds."

Maury sees his daughter stand, and her sock, at the top, is flecked with blood. He turns to the man in the fur hat. "She's bleeding. Your kid hit her so hard he drew blood. What do you have to say to that?"

The man in the fur hat looks over to the girl and frowns. He returns his gaze to Maury, hooded, made meaner by the fur hat pulled far over his brow. He shrugs.

"How'd you like it if I drew your blood?" Maury is a head taller than the other man—even with the ridiculous hat. Maury gives him a push, one hand in the chest. "What do you think of that? Can you say anything about that?"

The man steps back and continues to glare at Maury. Frat Ref waves back kids. Other parents start to stand on the bleachers, some beginning to talk, others calling for their kids. Maury pushes the man again. The man mutters something in Russian, Maury thinks.

"Don't fucking do that, talk to me in English, let me know what you have to say. I'd love to hear it."

The man looks to the side then, barks "Ura! Now!" He crosses his arms, looking up at Maury.

"What?" Maury says. "What? Say something before I knock the crap outta you."

"I am leaving now. Going. You do not see."

His son appears at his side, the little brute, his face white with concern. Maury sees the kid is skinnier than he first thought. He has purplish smears under his eyes, and his hair is too long, full of cowlicks. Maury looks back at the boy's father. He wants things he can only sense. He knows he is not doing this well, knows this is not how to resolve a conflict. He recognizes what he should do, but he can't do it. He feels it push like a stone in his eye. He says, "Good. Go. Fine," and watches them walk away.

The ref, having herded the children to their benches, now strides up. He gives Maury the speech and then bans him from future games, all things that do not surprise Maury. What does surprise him is how he has lost track of Kayla. He spins, and when he sees her, she is hunched at the end of her team's bench, picking at her shoes, and he can see from the angle of her head that she is near crying and, for a moment, so is he.

"I am not a monster," Maury says to Bunny, at home. "I know how it looks, but, I don't know, you just had to be there," he says. "I watched him the whole game, going after her—"

"Why didn't you say something earlier?"

"That's the ref's job. I didn't want to be one of *those* parents—"

"So you opted for being the THUG parent?"

He glares at her, and then she clasps her hands on top of her head.

"How does this even happen?" Bunny says. "Aren't you paid to resolve conflict? Aren't you supposed to be"—she makes air quotes—"a *dispute resolution specialist?*"

He holds his hands up. "Okay."

"Okay what?"

"Enough with that. You weren't there."

"Maybe, but I've been there plenty of times," Bunny says. "And I've seen her get roughed up before, but I've somehow managed not to be a goon about it."

"The little—he drew *blood*," Maury says.

Bunny casts her arms wide. "Yeah, so? That's what happens! It's sports! She loves to play, and, I think, she even likes getting rough. Jesus."

"Well, I don't like it, not a bit," Maury says.

"You're not the one in uniform."

They both stop talking. Her neck is flushed, from well below her collarbones up to the round knob of her chin. They grow aware of the television chatter at about the same time, and both look toward it. A weather front moves over the east coast, a cold front. The next game, it looks like, will be in the rain. Maybe it's good he's banned.

She says, then, "You know that guy who nearly killed that man at the hockey game? He's in jail now. And I am sure that is doing nothing in the role model department for his kid. And I am damn sure it wouldn't do anything for Kayla."

He frowns. "Come on, it wasn't that bad, two pushes. And he baited me."

She stands. "This is the last I am going to say on this," she says, pointing her finger near his face. "You are the adult. You're supposed to set an example and take care of your kid, and you did neither. You need to think about this, and think hard—"

"I don't need—"

"*Listen.* That's it. That's all I'm saying. I'll take her to soccer for a while. You will not let this happen again."

As she leaves the kitchen, he wants to call after her, to tell her he is already aware of the costs of what he's done. He knows he screwed up. He feels horribly. He just doesn't want to hear about it forever from her. Though, he thinks, if she lives up to her word, he won't. This will be the end of it and he will work through the atonement. Folding laundry without being asked. Going out for milk late at night. Remembering to put the seat down. A month of good behavior. *It's like a continuous childhood*, he thinks, this routine of good behaviors to atone and win back favor. It could be worse. He could have really snapped.

He thinks then of the man, his fur hat, his deep eyes, the pinch of hurt in his face. It must have been deeply humiliating and frustrating to have some goon all over him like that, with nothing to say back, no way to control the language his attacker was too quick to use. Maury was a big guy, and not the most handsome. Bunny'd told him many times that his nostrils twitch when he gets mad. How's that for a sight? You're in a fight in a foreign language, in front of your kid, and the goon yelling at you looks sleep-deprived and hasn't shaved in a few days, and on top of all the yelling and the spit flecks at the corner of his mouth, his red nose shivers at you, a little snot flutter of rage, coming at you. How do you just drive home after that? How do you explain to your son what happened? Yes, you kept your composure, but how do you explain that to a boy?

As it drizzles through the entirety of the next game, Maury sits in the Explorer, fiddling with the timing on the intermittent wipers, all the while peering to see what little of the game he can. He parked in the row closest to the fields, but Kayla's game

120

is on the second field in, so he has to look through one game to see hers. The ref from last time, looking, if possible, more disheveled, is calling the game closest to Maury, and looks at him during nearly every lull. Maury wants to get out of the truck just to see what the boy would do, but is also aware of Bunny, arms crossed in a lawn chair, one eye trained on being angry at him while the other watches their daughter. Maury can't see Ura, or his father.

He decides he will leave the truck after all, look around the parking lot, see if he can find out anything about the Russian. Sure, he was banned from the games, but that means what, exactly? No coming to the parking lot, or just no approaching the field, no sideline privileges? And based on what authority? The boy needed to make clear the terms. Maury had expected a call from the league manager, or one of the team parents, telling him in detail what his expulsion meant. Absent that call, or *any* follow-up, he now wonders whether it was just that the bonehead had seen one too many spirited ejections on *SportsCenter*.

As he strolls among the rows of cars, Maury wills himself not to look back. If he looks back, and meets Bunny's eyes, it will look as though he knew he was doing something wrong. He is not, so he won't give her the opening. If she's going to be pissed about this, she will have to get up, march over, and *tell him* she's pissed. All the cars look like they've been washed. They are all cleaner than his. In many cases, they are bigger than his: Expeditions, Excursions, Navigators, Escalades. The whole parking lot is an exercise in grandiose protection, carrying one's kids around in the suburban equivalent of a tank. Not much he could say, considering he bought his just so he could have a shot at life after a forced encounter with any them. But the main thing he thinks to himself is that the Russian would not own such a vehicle, most likely. He doesn't know why he senses it, but he does.

In the third row, he spots an older Volvo wagon. He strolls toward it, sees it covered in Sierra Club and Amnesty International stickers, and realizes it's not the Russian. The ref, maybe, or maybe the girl who is calling Kayla's game. Yeah, probably hers. He looks in the windows, sees a big mesh bag with two soccer balls in it, a gym bag, a single sock. Nods. He keeps going. He hears a long whistle blast, looks up, and sees Kayla's game just ended. He scans the parking lot, and sees an old Honda Civic, but it has a garter on the mirror. *That* is Frat Ref's car. So, no Russian. He didn't come. Maury pulls his hat down a bit lower on his brow. He had succeeded in keeping the man away, and is not sure how he feels about that.

He starts back toward the Explorer, and from the looks of things, Bunny did not realize he'd gone strolling. She is still on the field, helping Kayla get into a windbreaker, and talking with her coach. Maury glares at Frat Ref and strolls across the field toward the coach. Frat Ref looks like he's about to say something, but Maury holds out a hand, palm facing the boy, and nods, continuing to walk. It does the trick. By the time he reaches Bunny, however, Kayla's coach has already moved to join them.

"Mr. Platt, I understand you're not supposed to be on the field," he says. He crosses his arms, and Bunny sighs with vigor and gives Kayla a juice box.

"Game's over. I can be here now," Maury says. They look at one another. "I'm not here to do anything, just to collect everyone."

The coach presses his lips together. After a moment, he says, "You know, that man the other day, he didn't speak English, or not much anyway. He didn't understand, you know, what was going on."

"I know that," Maury says. "I tried to talk with him, a bit."

"That's not what that was," the coach says.

Maury tries to smile as he says, "I can do without you moralizing."

The coach holds his hands up. "No problem. Just trying to help."

Maury considers the truth of that for a second, and how he feels terrible about the situation, and wants to do something. After a pause, he says, "I should send the guy a fruit basket or something."

"That's not a good idea," the coach says. "You don't know how he'll take it. I'd just leave it."

In the car, Bunny agrees. "He's right, you need to let it drop. Just avoid him and make sure he doesn't try to sue us."

It hadn't occurred to him that he could be sued over this. It seems ridiculous to do so, but there it is. There were people who would do that. He did not, however, suspect the Russian of being that kind of person. He had only met this man once, and while he was maybe making too much of it, he felt like he knew him, already, simply from their exchange. It was an extreme exchange, a moment when people reveal more about themselves than they might in more socially confined encounters. And in the midst of the extremity, the Russian, unlike him, kept his composure, managed to avoid the fight. The Russian carried himself as one was supposed to in such situations. The Russian, he thus figured, was not litigious. And, perhaps, due to the language and cultural barrier, didn't realize one could redress such pettiness with the force of American civil law. Such an idea, Maury reasons, would be so novel to someone from the former

Soviet regime simply because of its glorification of individual desires as things worth preserving and, if thwarted knowingly, worthy of punishing the thwarter.

That night, after Kayla and Bunny have each gone to bed, he sits at the kitchen table with the phone book and starts looking. It's just not that big a town, he reasons, and a Russian name should just pop out. Anything ending in –vich. But after he is several pages into the Bs, he realizes it won't work. He has to figure out another way. He knows Bunny keeps the youth soccer papers in a file somewhere, and when he finds them, he brightens at the prospect of a directory or phone tree or something, and while he finds such documents, nowhere is there a name that seems right. He makes himself a cup of tea, squeezes out the bag with his fingers to wake himself up a bit, and then starts to really piece it out. He channel surfs on the small TV in the kitchen, and it hits him that the Russian works at either the college or the electronics manufacturer. Those were places in town that brought in foreigners. Now that he thinks he can track the man down, he wants even more to see him again.

He has a last surge of thought, and turns on the computer. He finds the website of the college and starts scrolling through pages in the engineering school. While looking through the faculty profiles in mechanical engineering, he sees the face. He almost didn't recognize him without the hat and because, in the picture, his hair is slicked down, almost as if gelled into place. Teodor Cuza is smiling, looking cartoonish, as though the photographer made him laugh. Maury wonders what it was that made the man smile like that, what joke cracked the façade.

Teodor's bio says he'd won an NSF fellowship, and thus didn't have to teach. He is working on a textbook for his specialization: the mechanics of heat. Maury thinks this is ironic. He clicks on the bio link, and sees more pictures, this time of the family, his wife, small boned and pointy-faced. The son, with his white face and bruised eyes. A shot of them on a bright green couch they most likely obtained as a second, since Maury could not imagine anyone he knew with such a couch in their house. And, it turns out, he is not Russian at all. He is from Romania, a place Maury knows of only because of the Olympics and gymnastics. He recalls the frailty of Nadia, of her miraculous tumbling, and the rumored barking she lived with as a communist athlete. He couldn't see Teodor screaming at his boy, yet Bela Karolyi had looked downright avuncular every time Maury saw him, so maybe.

When he finally sees the man's home address in the phone book, he slumps in his chair. The Cuza family lives exactly one street over, perhaps nearly behind his house, just on the other side of the thatch of hemlocks separating the two neighborhoods.

He doesn't sleep. He wants to drive over to the house, wants to learn more about them, but it is after midnight and he has a full slate the next day. A group of fundraisers coming in the morning for team building, and the mathematics department in the afternoon. Their head wants them to undergo some sensitivity training. As if Maury were in any position for such training. He imagines one of them as a soccer parent who, just as Maury reaches the zenith of the training session, whips out her phone with a video and starts yelling *Fraud! Fraud!* The woman then holds it up and lets them all see Maury's inadequacies. When he finally tries to sleep, he can't stop thinking about his daughter, hunched at the end of the bench, confused and withdrawn as her father yelled at a little man on the field.

The next morning, the fundraisers are boisterous, saving their most enormous argument for when they attempt, as a group, to define *consensus*. One woman is near tears and a bearded man storms from the room to stand outside until people "get real." Maury grows punchy with fatigue, and as lunch approaches, he resists the urge to herd them all together and yell at them, but when several people melt down over the variety of cheeses on the deli plate, he blows up. At the end of it, he is only paid half his fee, they leave an enormous mess in the dining area, and he thinks the group leaves more screwed up than when they arrived. He is tempted to call the mathematicians to tell them to hold off. But then he realizes, because the fundraisers left early, he has three hours before the math professors. One of the interns is already cleaning the dining area. He could drive to the Cuza's. Teodor was probably home—he was on a fellowship, didn't have to teach, had a book to write. He'd be around. Maury could say a few words to the man, make it right, and be back and better and ready to go. This could all go away.

He thinks about what Bunny would do. First, she would probably tell him not to go over there. But assuming she did, what would she do that would be just right? What little thing? He stops at Sheetz and prowls the Entenmann's rack, looking for a simple coffee cake, something nice but that wouldn't make anyone feel like they had to eat it right then. As he looks, he hears his own breathing, as if suddenly the piped-in music and the cooler hum and the rustling of other people went away, as if the world, for a moment, stopped to see what he would do, to listen to the crinkle of his windbreaker, feel the rush of heat in his forehead, let his worry warm the room.

When the door to the Cuza house opens, Maury smells something like licorice, only spicier, as if cooked with onions. Fennel, he realizes. He sees the wife then, whom he recognizes from the picture. She looks even smaller and sharper than the pictures suggested, all chin and elbows, tight eyes and a bony shoulder showing through a thin gray t-shirt. Her jeans look new, and ironed.

"Yes?"

His hands tingle, and his mouth goes dry. He holds the cake like a shield. "Is Dr. Cuza home?"

She cocks her head and her eyes flit to the cake and back to his face. "Are you a student of his?"

"No," Maury says. "I'm Maury. Maury Platt. I had a—a bad exchange with him last week, at soccer—"

Her neck twinges once, like a tendon meant to jump out at him. Otherwise, she does not move.

"It's okay, I just want to talk to him. I want to apologize. Say I'm sorry." He wants to keep talking, since she shows no intention of talking, but he doesn't know what to say. He wishes he had thought more about this, about what he would do. He sees a pair of small loafers near the door. The son.

"Is your son home? Because, really, I owe him an apology as well."

"Yes."

He thrusts out the cake. "And this is for all of you, just a cake, for, you know—"

"I'll put on coffee," she says, turning away from the door. She is gone quickly and, surprised, Maury steps into the house. Once inside the door, standing on old tiles in need of cleaning, he sees the green couch, two mismatched end tables, an elaborate chair, and a few black and white photographs in blonde frames. The photographs stick out, as if something purchased specifically to look like art. He can hear her in the kitchen, which sounds as if it is behind the wall where the couch sits, and he is not sure where he should sit, if at all. He steps into the living room and places the cake on an end table when the boy appears from a hallway off to the side.

The boy slows to a stop near the couch and looks at him. Maury presses his lips together and nods. The boy glowers, turns on one foot, and goes into the kitchen. Maury hears running water and a few harsh hisses.

The wife comes back into the room. "So, I am Elena, and this is Ura. Ura, this is Mr. Maury."

"Mr. Platt," he says, stepping forward and extending his hand. "Maury Platt."

Elena nods, puts a hand to her forehead and turns to look at her boy. Ura does not stick his hand out, only glowers at Maury.

"I don't know what I was expecting," Maury says, to no one in particular. Elena frowns and puts a hand on Ura's shoulder. Maury inhales once, crouches down so he can look at the boy, and knits his hands together in front of him.

"I'm sorry about the way I acted last week, young man, and I am ashamed of the way I behaved with your dad," he says in his best counselor voice. He hopes it sounds sincere enough. "I am also sorry about what I said about you, and I hope you don't let it get in the way of your enjoying yourself at games."

He stops, pleased with what he came up with off the cuff, though parts of it, he knew, were canned from some of the stuff he taught groups. Better they are put to this use, he thinks.

Ura looks up at his mother and worms out from under her shoulder. She tells him to be nice, and he says, "I don't have to be." Maury stands, and does so too quickly. He is dizzy, and the smell of the coffee hits him then, and the fennel, and he steps back, into a lamp he hadn't seen. He catches it before it falls over, and as he does so, Ura leaves the room. As Maury steadies the lamp, a door slams with a pock like hollow doors make.

"I'm sorry, I should really go," he says.

Elena looks down the hall, then back through the kitchen doorway. "You do not want coffee?"

Maury waves his hand at the hall. "He seems upset, still, no wonder, really. And I—I have work, and, maybe this was a bad idea."

She shakes her head. "No, it was a good idea. You are right to apologize."

He is not sure if she is rebuking or congratulating him. Her voice is almost monotone, and not as halting as her husband's, but lacks much inflection. He looks into her face, but still can't decide how to take the remark. It doesn't matter; she's right, whatever her meaning.

"I'm glad you think so."

They both stand in the living room as they hear the coffee maker's final hiss and gurgle. He wants to go, before the kid comes back out, before the two of them fight or turn against him, before it all goes south. He can tell she has an unreasonable need to give him the coffee. He has a travel mug in the Explorer, so maybe she will give it to him to go.

"I can do that," she says. "You get the cup."

Outside, the street is quiet. He can see his own chimney, several houses down, poking up above the hemlocks at the end of his yard. He smells cut grass, odd in mid-week. The air seems cleaner, cooler, less stuffy than the Cuza house.

In the narrow kitchen, she smiles at his travel mug as he hands it to her.

"My husband loves these things," she says, turning it over as though it were a seashell. "He talks about them when teaching, about how they work, their thermal properties. They are very American. Crafty."

Maury shrugs. Coffee mugs. Wonder of technology. Space age thinking. She is inordinately happy about it, grinning as she fills the cup, still grinning as she hands him a carton of cream. As he stirs the coffee, he hears the front door open and quickly close. When he looks up, he startles Teodor Cuza.

"Elena," Teodor yells. "Elena where are you?"

She pushes past Maury and out into the living room. She begins talking to her husband in another language, very quickly. He closes his eyes tightly and shakes his head. He keeps saying something that sounds to Maury like *nyet. Nyet nyet.*

Finally, he steps past her and points to Maury. "Get out of my house."

"I came to apologize," Maury says. He holds his arms to his side, makes himself as open as he can. "I brought you all a cake."

Teodor's eyes focus on the travel mug, then the coffee pot. He turns to Elena, then back to Maury.

He nods, his jaw clenching twice. He jabs a finger. "Coffee good?"

"Listen, I just wanted to say—"

"I don't care. Not here. Not—this is not the place." His voice rises. "You do not come to my house, talk to my family, when I am not here." He chops at the air. "You do not."

"I thought you would be here, I don't know. Look, I'm sorry."

"Get out. Get out of my house, you—you shit."

Maury has to walk right past Teodor to leave, and as he does so, he does not expect the man to move out of his way. He even expects a shoulder, a lean in, but instead, Teodor bows his head slightly and steps to the side. Maury thinks how Teodor is handling this so much better than he had. When he steps out the front door, he hears a video game loudly through an open window, probably the son's. He turns toward the noise, and he sees the back of the boy's head through the window, sees it twitch from side to side, his hair in high relief against a television screen in front of him, the image like a corona, something immensely hot and pressing.

In the Explorer, he pokes at the radio's seek button, hustling through stations searching for something different to listen to. He stops on what he thinks is James Brown, only to realize after a mile or so that it is a sermon. The man on the radio, mimicking the Godfather of Soul, chants on and on about the fire of the soul, and Maury enjoys the rhythm and the repetition of the message, the incantation. He does not want to have to see Teodor Cuza again, but he will, now, almost surely. At every game from here on, Maury will instinctively find the face. He curses at drivers moving too slowly, and once he is back at work, he can feel he needs an antacid.

The facility is empty, and none of the other team members are anywhere in the building. He suspects most are outside. In his office, he looks at the posters and aphorisms on his walls, the gentle words of sober behavior. He pictures himself tearing the posters down in a mad rush, then thinks about actually getting up and doing it—not in great seething motions, but calmly, taking pieces of tape off the posters, rolling them into tubes, placing them between the wall and a filing cabinet, saving them for the day when he might put them back up, when he might not feel such a hypocrite looking at them.

He tells himself he's being precious, and it's not helping anyone. He picks up the phone and starts to dial Bunny, but what, exactly, would he tell her? That he stalked the guy, visited his family, freaked out his kid, made small talk with the wife until the guy got home to feel again emasculated, and then let Cuza throw him out of the house? Not a good strategy.

He picks up his desk coffee mug, ceramic and cold, the middling contents nearly congealed, and he tells himself what he is about to do will be the end of it. Then he cocks his arm and hurls the mug against the cinder block wall. The mug's destruction is not loud, just forceful, with pieces everywhere that take Maury a long time to find.

For about an hour that night, he lays next to Bunny, trying to make himself sleep. He tries to remember different meditation exercises, but just as he starts to work one, he thinks about the intended effects, ways he might suggest the application to others, and before long his thoughts turn to meta-meditation, and he annoys himself until he tosses. Each time he shifts, Bunny rasps or grunts. At the end of the hour, he goes to the kitchen. His stomach knots and knots. He watches TV to make himself tired and, when he awakens the next morning, feels worse. His face and forehead feel clammy, and he wonders if he has a fever.

Woozy with fatigue, he drives to the convenience store by the high school fields. The morning fog has the grass so wet it lays

down in spots under the bleachers where it is still long. He emp-
ties his travel mug, pouring Elena's coffee onto the grass, shaking out the last drops. He thinks about them, about how they
are probably still asleep, about how they go to the soccer game
later in the morning, how Teodor might wonder if the ugly gi-
ant will come after him again, ham-fisted with apologies and at-
tempts at reconciliation. He will worry about the boy, too, about
how Ura is fitting in, whether he still enjoys the game, all of it,
all of the same things Maury worries about for Kayla.

He can feel that the day will be warm, and he can feel his
stomach rumbling and gurgling. In spite of both, he fills the
mug with coffee and drives home.

Later, at the game, he sees Elena. She is the only woman in the
80-degree heat wearing a scarf on her head. She also wears sun-
glasses. He wonders about the get up, laughs to himself that she
looks like a woman in a movie on *Lifetime*, and then shudders.
He works through the other parents and walks down the sideline
toward the bleachers where she sits. Bunny is two fields away, at
the game where he cannot be. Frat Ref is working that game,
and there would be no way for him to sneak up there. Down
here, Rain or Sunbeam or Dandelion or whatever her name is
calls the game, and she doesn't know Maury. The one person
who does see him is the boy, Ura, playing fullback again, whose
eyes lock onto Maury. Maury waves but the kid does nothing.

When he gets close enough to look at Elena clearly yet without being seen, he studies her face. He can't find any evidence
of bruising or cuts, and while he feels silly and terrified at doing
such a thing, he can't shake the idea that maybe Teodor hit her
after he left. He could see what the man's logic would be—to
let Maury in was to undermine his resolve, other macho crap.

Maury imagines he hears Bunny's retort: *you're not one to talk about who gets to act out of macho crap instincts.*

He looks at her, even squints, until he sees Teodor stand up. Maury turns away as quickly as he can. When he glances back, he sees Teodor stretch once and then offer his hand to help Elena stand. The two step down the bleachers as Maury realizes the game is over. He looks toward Kayla's field and sees her and Bunny striding toward the Explorer. He doesn't know which way to go.

Then, Teodor is near him, walking just ten feet from him. He cradles Elena's elbow, as gently as he would an egg, and he glares at Maury. Elena turns her head away and Maury is not sure, will never be sure, if he saw a bruise or not. He opens his mouth, wants to stop them so he can figure out what he can do to make things right, what new words he can put together to take it all back. But as his mouth opens and closes, they pass by, and soon Ura runs to them. Teodor hugs the boy across the shoulders, and Elena laughs. He turns to watch them walk to their car, and as he does, he sees Bunny and Kayla beyond them.

Kayla pulls at her jersey, and she is talking but not looking at her mother. Bunny's lips press together. If it is possible to be dismissive with hips, she is managing it. Maury feels immersed then in a bubble of nausea. His forehead glistens and then beads as he jogs toward one of the porta-potties. He doesn't have time to go inside, and instead leans forward, an arm holding him up, and he heaves twice at the side of the stall. He lets his head hang for several seconds, spitting a few times, trying to will the taste from his mouth. He lets his forehead rest against the wall. He is, for the moment, cool.

Unemployed

As she puts the receiver in the cradle, she knows how she will change: in the coming week, she will cancel the cable, the paper, and the Internet. Her son will whine that she has an iPhone and she will tell him, while at the breakfast table before school, already four cigarettes into a two-pack day, that it costs less than the land line. And she needs the phone for jobs. She won't tell him she also needs it to call his father and defend her actions. By the end of two weeks, she will have them eating pasta, beans and rice, tuna fish. She will fantasize about pizza. She'll avoid smoking near him, since his father will have told him to holler "Forty-two cents!" every time he saw one. One night, he will pass her to get some juice, and he will yell it, and she will sting with the need to hit him. He will look at her as if she had. She will sit up later that night and want to call someone, but will think of a damned good reason not to call each person. Her sister would lecture, work her way toward a conversation about Jesus. Her husband would act like jobs are pets, go to the SPCA and get one. Her one friend at work would be awkward, and say she had to get off the phone. One friend's sympathy will overwhelm and the other will dig in her own history to find the example showing she's had it worse. By the end of the month she will still not have a job, and while her old job will have stopped challenging the claim for unemployment, the checks will barely cover even the lean version of their new lives. She will reconsider waitressing, fast food, cleaning hotel rooms, scams to make rent. She will wonder what mandates she do more than persist. She will smoke in the one bar left where she can. She will watch people pass. She will flick ashes into a paper boat made from the classifieds. Her son will speak less, and she will put off getting him a haircut because they are too expensive and she is not sure she can do it herself. Every time he brushes his hair from his face, she feels a fingernail scratch inside her sternum. One thing she does not see: the end, a call from one of her friends, the conversation leading to a lunch with a woman wearing glasses and a beige suit. She does not see the lunch, crabcakes, an extravagance of salad. She does not see how, a few days later, she will sit in the corner of a barber shop, amid young men sleepy with mid-day, her eyes running with tears behind a copy of *Golf Digest*, her legs itching from new hose, her entire chest yearning for a cigarette, while her son laughs at the barber's dumb jokes, again and again.

GROUNDSCRATCHERS

The Jesus Boys are back. Like last summer, they eat tuna hoagies and Snapple Peach at the Super-Wawa. They talk about girls, laugh like other boys. But from beneath lowered bills of baseball caps, they also argue scripture and translation matters. In baggy jeans, they debate the apocrypha. Sometimes one will write on his forearm with a pen, another will have eyes dark with lack of sleep, but they are civil, and while they debate morals and merit, they seldom moralize.

Their reappearance means it has been a year since Yoshi. Almost a year since the last time I drove under the beeches at Copper Beech Farm. Jocelyn would find it funny, if she still spoke to me, that I am finally able to remember a date of significance.

I was the supervisor of grounds for Albert Wynn's largest single property, Copper Beech Farm, and the gem he loved most of all his baubles. Wynn is as fickle as he is eclectic. He has bred dogs and horses, bought and sold wine, developed and sold two high-tech businesses, presided over a savings and loan, run a trio of restaurants on the Main Line, and, for three semesters, taught classics at Haverford. His grandfather had been an investor in several Philadelphia utilities and railroads, and established a trust for his sole grandchild that came to fund Wynn's single enduring passion: his amenities.

The trust paid me for the decade I served Wynn. And I had done a creditable enough job to be mentioned in regional newspapers, including the *Philadelphia Inquirer*. I coordinated the efforts to mow the sixty-four acres of lawn, hay or burn the forty acres of meadow, manage the forest on the remaining 130 acres, and maintain the three ponds. I oversaw pruning, garden development and maintenance, snow removal, hardscape installation and upkeep, and related incidentals. I was dedicated: I had run a landscape business for a decade prior to service with Wynn, and in the last months of my time at Copper Beach, even sacrificed my marriage for him. Jocelyn would claim I sacrificed *her*—a claim I'm not comfortable fighting.

Two years ago, at a party in the Hamptons, Wynn was given a copy of *New York Times Sunday Magazine* in which he read the story of one Yoshi Higashide, a self-proclaimed specialist in Zen Fusion gardening, a maximal minimalist, the man who transformed floral abundances along Long Island Sound into muted spaces—ruddy, splotchy lawns terminating in rocks, sycamore trunks in fog, pencil lines of water cutting through beds of black stones.

And so Yoshi arrived that June, driving an Audi and wearing a Hawaiian shirt, jeans, combat boots, and wire-rimmed glasses, his hair slicked into rows of thin spikes. He stood by his car, looking at the tops of the beeches framing the drive. I assumed he was lost. I cut the power to the trim mower and he shouted

Wynn's name, his accent heavily Japanese.

"He's at the main house, there is a receptionist there," I said.

"You work on the lawn?" The fingernails on his left hand were polished black.

"Yes," I said.

"You cut too high, and you need to change your pattern more. I see ruts from here," he said, pointing out into the lawn.

I varied the pattern every time, used the finest British-manufactured reel mower available in the states. I sharpened the blades prior to every cut.

"I'll take it under advisement."

He shook his head. "No. You will do it. This drive must disappear because the lawn look so good."

"I'm Michael Petrin, the grounds supervisor." I extended my hand and he looked at it for a second before giving it a surprisingly sturdy shake.

"We will work well together, I can tell," he said. I had no idea if he was joking. "I am Yoshi Higashide, and Mr. Wynn call me to work on this place, to update it."

The breeze picked up, and I heard grasses ticking along the rise behind the drive, the shiver of beech leaves. I turned from him and looked at the gentle swells, the trunks of birch and oaks rising out of the cool grass, the bank of sedge and pampas cresting the hill, the neat pea gravel of the drive, natural rhythms in controlled expression. Beyond the swell, the flat roof of the fieldstone house sliced the horizon, the mountains a slate purple behind it. How could he possibly *update* such a view?

"Well, Yoshi, it's the first I hear of it. We should talk."

He grinned, pointed to his temple. "I thought of everything. We'll be fine. I have drawings. I will provide you help for setting up a proper maintenance program."

My chest tightened. I wanted to talk to Wynn.

That was a year ago. The camp upstream had opened, and little Baptist girls and boys had come to talk with the Jesus Boys, to become enlightened while learning to be proper stewards of God's green earth. Part of my charge was to leave my quarters each night and patrol the back meadow and woods, where Wynn's land abutted the camp, to make sure camp kids, filled with talk of the lord, weren't out humping or drinking in the meadow. Jocelyn thought I should go easy, thought Wynn was being stuffy. *The summers are theirs*, she would say, *to learn about passion and risk and daring*. I said, *better they outgrow that now*. Given what she had endured, I found her attitude both brave and sanctimonious. I sought to say things that would annoy her, perhaps because I found myself cowardly in comparison.

But on my own, in the fields as I did what I was asked and reasserted order over Wynn's property, each couple I chased off with a flashlight made me wonder what damage they were doing, and why a guy who bred dogs and horses didn't have at least a little respect for the forces at work at that age, in that camp. He would only invoke insurance as just cause.

Wynn was to leave for Australia for several weeks, and while he was gone, Yoshi would use the main house. Wynn came to my cottage the night before he left and said, unconvincingly, he had told me about Yoshi. The only mention I remember was when he said he might entertain some drawings for the main house, where a storm had taken out an ancient birch. I wanted to do the design, but was behind that spring due to rain, so figured if he wanted to try out some local, that was fine. How that bal-looned into Yoshi I hardly understand. How it wound up with Yoshi living in his home is baffling.

I promised Wynn I would direct the guys to work with Yoshi, make tools and equipment available, and even review resumes and references of contractors. But Wynn would have to make it clear I was grounds supervisor, that I did not work for Yoshi, and that major changes needed my approval. Wynn waved his hands, said "Of *course*" a half-dozen times, took a long last draw on the beer I'd offered him, asked me to say hello to "Joyce," and then stepped off my porch as if the conversation had been about the Phillies.

I know I told her about Yoshi afterward. My certainty comes because it is the last image of her that stays with me. When I try to call her to mind now, it is the back of her head I see, the tired curl of her hair squeezed into a clip, its russet color still rich, its length returning, and her treating it as a nuisance. Surely, it got in the way for her—it's why she had cut it off initially after her injury. But over the years, as she went back to the hairdressers, she had them leave it a little longer each time. That night, I noticed it was almost as it was, that her shoulders were square again, that her neck had appeared to lengthen, holding her head high again. That night, she looked younger, though the blue light of her monitor still blasted her features to a pale draw, and though her voice had more depth to it. In the moment, I thought she had agreed with me that Yoshi would be trouble, but later I wondered if she didn't just tell me to relax.

I woke the next morning to the smell of char. I jogged across the south lawn, half-dressed, worried the trees were on fire. An angry sputter of smoke pushed above the beeches. I broke into a sprint.

Past the beeches, Yoshi sat cross-legged before an enormous pyramid of flame. His bonfire was in the lawn fronting the house.

I yelled, "What is this?"

He swiveled toward me, glaring.

"Please, not now."

"Put out the fire."

He sliced a hand at me.

I looked at my watch. It was still 6:30. No one would be at the landscape building for another half hour.

"Either put it out or tell me what's—"

He sliced a hand at me again. I strode to the landscape building. I opened the irrigation grid and flipped on the sprinkler heads. I waited.

It took him longer than I thought. He probably had to figure out someone could actually turn on the irrigation, and then had to learn where the landscape building was, with no one there but me to tell him. He arrived soaked, but strangely serene.

"You need to talk to me," I said. "Keep me in the loop."

He folded his hands together, arms straight, and shuffled his feet out to shoulder width, like he was getting in his argument stance.

"I am in charge of the new plan, and things must be done, first steps."

"I am in charge of the grounds, and when there are fires on the grounds, things must be done."

He nodded, inhaled deeply, and said, "For the plan to proceed, the energy must be correct."

I nodded. I had no idea what he was getting at, but I could be reasonable.

"I was performing a very important task," he said, then he paused, as if seeking the right words. "I needed to clean the energy."

"Clean the energy," I said. I nodded again.

"The fire, it is built of certain things, to purify, to clean."

"Okay," I said. "But to me, it looks like a fire. You didn't tell me the plan." I stood and set the irrigation grid back to its schedule. "Does Wynn know part of the job included burning holes in his lawn?"

"That lawn will go," he said.

I nodded. I felt like a bobblehead. "Okay, maybe, we'll get to that one. But does Wynn know you are starting fires, and whatever else?"

"He knows what I do. I tell him how. There are rites, meditation, other things."

"You have to tell me, too. Let me know," I said.

He looked at me like I had kicked his dog. "I will tell what you need to know."

"Fair enough. Just know you might not always know what I need to know."

He nodded then, a sharp head-butt to the air.

What is the worst thing one person can do to another? Not physical violence. The human spirit has a healthy record of mending. Jocelyn had her arm hacked off by a burglar twelve years ago. A drug addled man with a machete attacked her while robbing a gas station. He wanted the cash at the register, she didn't move fast enough, he started flailing. He hit her three times—two cuts, one superficial across her abdomen, one deep on her right arm, then the chop that took her left forearm. Within a year, she typed faster than anyone I knew. Granted, I didn't know many people who typed, but still. You also don't see many one-armed typists. On top of that, she started a blog for amputees, raised money through said blog to help people afford prostheses, and made friends with an army of slower typists around the world. She made much more of chaos and tragedy than I ever could have.

Neither is betrayal the worst you can do. She recovered from that as well. She told me my betraying her was worse than what the attacker did. For years I believed her. She had suspected another woman, and despite the lack of evidence, with no connections romantic or otherwise, and my assurances that other women, real or imagined, had nothing to do with it, she maintains her theory, to the point that she accounts for the lack of presence of that woman by saying it went sour once she realized I could *leave a desperate amputee on her own*! But rage gave her purpose, even though my crimes, of adultery anyway, were imagined. Betrayal is not the worst thing one person can do to another. Betrayal can give purpose and remarkable focus as easily as it can bring you to your knees.

Disregard is the worst thing you can do. To utterly ignore someone, render them insignificant, not worth any extremity of response, any response at all. To make someone worthless. It obviates any power of reaction; you can't react to nothing, especially when anything you do fails to provoke any response. When what you do seems not to cause the slightest wrinkle. Only now I recognize that, given what Yoshi has done. Worse, I realize disregard was the true crime I committed against Jocelyn: I ran a business into the ground while ignoring her, then achieved success at the farm while ignoring her, and ultimately battled Yoshi while not even noticing that she disappeared.

She naturally felt betrayed when I ceased to notice her, and as she sought reasons, she latched on to one she could understand. It sounds patronizing, but perhaps that's the effect of advancing theories about others without them around to gainsay your ideas.

And through that summer, as the fields grew fecund with the nocturnal rompings of the Jesus Boys' charges and the plant count on the grounds of Copper Beech both grew and diversified, and as the tasks and worries that occupied my waking thoughts seemed to ramble like wild vetches, and as the sky lost the clear adolescent blue of spring for the white-gray heat of summer's murk, I found little evidence of Jocelyn. Looking back, it makes sense—more trips for *the cause*, more meetings with different medical and charitable organizations, more appearances to speak and gesticulate to the families of loved ones running 5K races with one or more fewer appendages than they were born with—and less time arguing with me, less time spent in our rented and shambling house, fewer words wasted on ears that would not hear them.

Wynn's receptionist, Alice, carried a torch for me. I'm not sure why. We have little in common. She got her degree at Bryn Mawr in history and went directly into this job because her father is a lawyer who knows Wynn. She is pretty, though not confident. Her skin is clear, her hair straight and never styled beyond a hair band or a pony tail, and her eyes have a downturn at the edges that make her look tired, sad, or thoughtful. She is probably fifteen years younger than me and would, if she had any sense of her talents at all, be an overachiever somewhere far from here. While not ambitious, she has done everything right in her life so far, with little effort and a natural ease, something I can't claim.

Yet, she made a point of smiling at me. She asked questions to prolong our conversations. She might not even have realized how she felt, or that she was just lonely, since the only people she saw most days were Wynn, me, the cook, or Yoshi. The crew weren't allowed near the house, and Wynn's driver seldom came in. She didn't make personal calls, so perhaps her interest was simply a natural outgrowth of loneliness.

A month after the fire incident, after Yoshi had torn up the six-year-old cottage gardens I had installed around the main house, I played my advantage with Alice and asked about Yoshi. I disliked him intensely, obviously, but thought he must be marginally credible, since he had high profile clients and his work was reviewed in respectable places. I even thought maybe it was me. Maybe I just didn't get it. Thing is, I did get a thing or two. I had run my business and read about my field, and while I didn't focus on Zen gardeners, I'd read a great deal about Asian influence. I had seen other properties, visited botanical gardens, taken a personal interest in my livelihood. Yoshi's approach did not add up.

After scorching the lawn, he studded the expanse with Japanese blood grass and planted plugs of bindweed to fill. He told me the use of weed material as a foundation plant was ironic. Further, he favored the chevron leaves of the plant, and assured me that the result, from a distance, would be to flatten with elaborate texture, and that the lawn would surprise with its irony while maintaining a Zen congruity. I let that slide.

Then, he planted fifteen Katsura trees in a circle, each root ball touching the other, entirely too close. He said the ones meant to be there would live, and that the fallen trunks of the others would suggest age and decay alongside the vigorous life of the remaining stalwarts. "And the circle," he said, holding his arms out, eyeing me like a co-conspirator. "You know, the circle?" I let that one slide, too.

He kept pushing it: he planted a checkerboard of grasses, alternating gold Molina with dwarf red fountain grasses. Every so often, he placed a big rock in one of the spaces that should have had a grass. Elsewhere, he wrapped chicken wire around the trunks of a dozen zelcova trees and coated the cages in concrete. Then painted them lemon yellow. He planted the courtyard near the house in moss and rocks, which was more like what I expected, but then showed up with a plaster reproduction of the Venus de Milo and a pavement saw. He chopped the torso off the statue, hollowed the interior with a cement drill and chisels, planted enormous dahlias in it, and jammed it, crooked, into the middle of the mossy expanse. On that day, I said to Alice, "I may be out of line, and tell me if it's none of my business, but how much are we paying him?"

Her eyes widened and she looked over her shoulder. The window behind her overlooked the courtyard, the Venus de Dahlias framed within it. Her face was like the peal of a bell.

I said, "What are you thinking?"

She pointed to the window. "Mr. Wynn is—I don't think he'll like this."

"Neither do I," I said.

She put a finger on her lip, then put both hands on the desk. "Should I call him?"

"Have you seen the Zelcova behind the ponds?"

"The yellow ones? Yes."

She wanted to laugh; I watched it worm through her. I wanted her to laugh, but I also wanted to know what, exactly, Wynn was paying. I tried to look severe. I even crossed my arms. But that overdid it. She started laughing, really hard.

"What the fuck is up with this guy?" she said. Then she covered her mouth. My surprise must have shown.

"I don't know. I want to find out what he did to get Wynn to give him such license, or if Wynn even has any idea," I said.

"No, I'd say he didn't."

"Why do you say that?"

"I heard him tell someone how he hired Yoshi to update the place *a little*. I don't know—the way he said it, it didn't sound so drastic."

"Did he say what the fee was?"

She smirked. Maybe I revealed myself as small, or maybe she enjoyed this sudden alliance. But after Alice looked through things I was sure she shouldn't, I learned Yoshi Higashide's day rate was roughly my monthly rate: five grand. Five grand a day for a disemboweled Venus and a grove of yellow trees.

I e-mailed Wynn in Australia. I enumerated Yoshi's offenses and asked what action to take. I took time ordering the paragraphs to sound rational and professional, aware as I was of the degree of my anger and how it might play out in e-mail. I offered short-term fixes to make some use of Yoshi's plantings while removing more offensive things, like the concrete tree casings and Venus. His response? I wasn't *giving Yoshi time for his vision to coalesce*. I wasn't *patient with the new aesthetic*. I had to, he wrote, *take time to appreciate the artistry in what, at first, are contradictory elements in the new landscape.* Wynn actually put that in the e-mail. This was a guy who referred to his stallions as Humpsters.

I suspected he got his new facility with language from the grand bullshit artist ensconced in his house. Yoshi's revivalist salesmanship was what they had at the Baptist camp, only instead of reaping windfalls peddling sin and loathing, Yoshi sold the emperor's new landscape. And, before sending his e-mail, I am sure the emperor himself ran it by the master. The master, whose written language skills dwarfed his spoken presentation, provided a reply well-worded and insulting in its brevity, its implied *just you wait, idiot.* I sought more, some critique, some failure.

The one person I found who dared criticize the man noted his landscapes lacked any sense of time passing, of maturing into something grander than what was first installed. None of his works were for the ages in the way landscape architects have, since Olmstead and Brown, sought to make them. The woman writing, an urban planner at MIT, cited as particularly brutal a hatchet job he did on Cape Cod: an eight foot curtain of steel cut off a front yard from its ocean view. Behind the curtain, Yoshi had installed a bed of iron gray gravel, studded with the twisted forms of dead dogwoods. He called it "Contemplative Field of Gray." The writer mentioned the steel got so hot in the summer that people's pets had actually been burned when brushing against it. Yoshi was paid $100,000 for it. The critic concluded by deriding Yoshi as a purveyor of "smashmouth landscaping: bowl-you-over installations with little care for whatever happened next." I made plans to ask Yoshi about it.

A few days afterward, I found him sitting cross-legged, wearing a t-shirt and pink billowy pants, near the checkerboard of grasses. Already, the expanse was shot with weeds, mostly sweetgrass. I asked if he wanted me to have a guy weed it.

"There are no weeds," he said, "just different intentionalities."

"Just asking," I said. "I have three guys who can help you, trained landscapers, all you got to do is ask."

He snorted. "Landscapers. They are just groundscratchers." He raked at the air with his fingers.

"You know, I'm trying to give you some help," I said. "You may want to make it work. Wynn will be back soon, and"—I gestured to the field—"he might not react the way you think he will."

He stood and brushed the back of his thighs, almost smiling. "It will be fine. I sent him photos with my phone. He is very happy." He patted me on the shoulder. "You should not worry."

I looked at the pattern and wondered how crazy Wynn was getting. Then I said, "What happened with that steel thing on Cape Cod?'

He grinned broadly. "You have been reading."

"What I read wasn't nice."

His grin persisted, as if pasted to his face. "That happens sometimes."

"People's pets were getting burned."

"We fixed that. We tore out the sidewalk, installed sedges and fescues. No problem."

"That's not the only thing—"

He swiped a hand in front of me. "I know what you read. She knows nothing. She plans cities—put building here, road there. That is nothing like what I do." He shook his head. "Hey, when you want to know what is for dinner, do you ask me, or ask the cook?"

"The cook doesn't cook for me. You know that's not the point."

"Maybe, but let me say: if I need someone to dig the hole or to cut the lawn, I will call you or your crew," he said. "Otherwise, leave me alone to work."

Weeks passed. The June rains stopped. As July approached, I held back on cutting the lawn because it was so dry. Jocelyn spent time visiting her therapist, traveling more. On the rare occasion I noticed she was home, she was more a noise, rapid-fire typing on her keyboard in the back of the house somewhere. When I went to Wawa for a late sandwich, the Jesus Boys lingered, soaking in the AC, putting off the return to the scorch. Even Yoshi slowed his installations, not wanting to over-tax the wells, a move I interpreted as concession to prudence. The crew maintained equipment, sharpening blades on pruners and saws, giving mowers and Gators oil changes, cleaning shovels and rakes. They gathered beer bottles from the meadow. They kept a Post-It note in the landscape building where they made hash marks for every condom found. As the weather grew warmer and drier, the hash marks multiplied, and I realized I'd have to make a few night patrols.

Of course, I put it off. Two nights before Wynn was to arrive, when I finally took to the fields, I sat up for the hour or two before my walk, sipping coffee on my porch. The house was quiet, even the tapping of keys quiet with Jocelyn somewhere in New England raising money. All I could hear were peepers from the ponds—the humidity and heat were so stilling I did not hear even the rustle of leaves—as though the farm were pillowed. I didn't want to walk—it was hot, I was happy on the porch, I wanted to be awake the next day. But I needed to let them know we were watching.

The paths made little sound. Once I made it to the meadow, the sky opened and it became easier to breathe. The moon over the meadow made grasses deep with shadow and illuminated stalks, a rolling expanse of bristling silver. A beech glowed on a small rise. I cut the flashlight to enjoy the moon's intensity, and strolled to the beech.

The meadow's lure was profound, and I wanted to sit. I had come to value such moments, as I had realized only in recent months that they were also something of a gift from Jocelyn. I did not realize how I preferred to be alone until she started travelling so much, and then I discovered the gift of open space, moments that could expand upon one another, like vistas in a garden, space where trees and plants had not closed in, where the imagination could seek the next progression, or simply dwell in the new space.

I was almost ready to stop, to give in to the meadow, when I heard a soft and almost rhythmic brush of grass. I stepped through the meadow grass and up the low swell near the beech. As my sight cleared the grass, the moon illuminated the athletic shoulders of a young man. He was bare to the waist, and his jeans fell to a bunch just below the cleft of his ass. I realized then that the noise I heard were huffs of breath coming from the girl kneeling in front of him. Her hands cupped the backs of his knees, and with each thrust of his hips, she exhaled loudly through her nose.

I stood as still as I could. She pulled back then and, in one quick motion, turned and bent to present herself to him. The moon made her glow like his shoulders, paler than she could possibly be by day, softer in her contours, less real in that light.

I swallowed hard. My chest hurt, and my eyes stung. I stood there, surprised how I hoped they didn't see me, hoped they wouldn't stop. I gripped the flashlight. One click and it would be over. I bit my lower lip and willed myself not to break down right there. Something in their rawness, the unreality and close magic of it, I missed. It wasn't Jocelyn or sex or love or anything like it—it felt most like missing the closeness of the unexpected, the openness to life and the willingness to receive it.

Controlling my life had meant I eliminated what every gardener works hard to cultivate: surprise. Texture. Serendipity.

After I turned and left, I passed Yoshi's latest improvement. East of the main house, past my own quarters, he had excavated a trench and filled it with bamboo. The effect was akin to an English ha-ha, fence and merger of the distant landscape to the one cultivated on the property. The twist was the emergence of the bamboo, seemingly dwarfed, uneven in its reach, tropical in a temperate field. I worried that if one pruned the bamboo too harshly, the gaping ditch would pose a hazard. I had amused and enraged myself with the thought that if Yoshi did make such a mistake, he would dismiss it as introducing "tension" to the landscape.

The bamboo shifted in a push of wind, the sound like the harsh breath of the girl in the meadow. I picked up the pace.

Over their hoagies the next day, the Jesus Boys discussed Christ's cursing of the fig tree. The tallest one, the one with the beard who actually looked like one of the Hasidim, told the group that the tree, though cursed, was not chopped down. It withered from the act of faith, and that faith could destroy if God saw such a wish as fitting. The other boys looked at him as though he had drawn a gun.

I thought, if only I were not a heathen, I could cause Yoshi's work to wither with faith. Or, better, if he were perceived as a sinner it would work on its own. I imagined the non-groves bursting into flames, bees teeming from the gutted torso of Venus' a graven image, or goat entrails percolating up from the beds of weeds—all the while the lithe thrashing of the camp kids in their wild fornicating would be like a sea amid which Yoshi's isle of torment festered. How would he ever explain it to Wynn?

Worse, how would he explain any kind of destruction, however mild, to Wynn?

The Jesus boys argued about the savior's intent, what some saw as the arrogance in cursing a creation of God. As they argued, I thought of cursing a creation myself. The day passed at a clip. While the crew skimmed muck from the pond surfaces, I sharpened hedge trimmers. While they cleaned their tools, I chatted with Alice regarding Wynn's return and the time he was expected the next day. While the crew drove off at day's end, I brewed a pot of coffee and took a call from Jocelyn—she was staying in Tucson (*Tucson?*) for a few more days. As she explained what I had forgotten and would not at that point remember either, I watched Alice's old Audi leave a languid dust rising over the drive as she left. I mentally reviewed the route and steps I would take. When Yoshi's light finally extinguished, I set an alarm for 1 a.m. and laid out on the couch.

It did not take as long as I had anticipated, nor did it make as much noise. Sharpening the trimmers had been the right move, as they made a neat snick through each hard shaft of bamboo. The tops fell in rigid alignment with their bases, sticking in the mud below, with the unintended effect of making the planting look thicker, drawing more emphasis to the level top line I created with the pruning. When I stepped back afterward, the ditch had only the slightest line of bamboo above it, cut severely to match the lawn stretching out on both sides. It looked completely nonsensical.

By noon, I still had not seen nor heard Yoshi. I stayed in the landscape building, compiling an order of replacement parts for the irrigation system. I stayed at my desk, my view taking in the lawn leading to the main house, my quarters, the new bamboo ditch, and the drive. If Yoshi entered the area to work, I would see him. He never did.

Just after noon, Wynn's limousine tore up the drive. I told the crew I would meet Wynn at the main house. While I hadn't said much about Yoshi to them, they weren't stupid. They knew confrontation was possible. One of them swept the same dirt near the front of the tractor bay several times as I prepared to walk to the main house.

Wynn was a bluster of hair and newly whitened teeth. "Michael, the place looks—" he spread out his arms, sport coat bunching at his neck, making his head appear smaller than usual—"challenging. It challenges me. Challenges my spirit and my, you know." He rolled his hands. "The sense of things, how they look—"

"Your aesthetic."

"Yes," he breathed. "Yes, exactly. This is great." He nodded, hands now on his hips. He inhaled deeply. "To be back, to drive under the beeches. Yes. Great."

He stared at the ditch with the sawn bamboo.

"How much do you know about what he's doing?"

"Hard to say, Al," I said.

He looked at me like I had said *befuddled porpoise* or something. After a second, he returned his look to the ditch. As he did, Yoshi emerged from it. My heart lurched.

"Mister Wynn!" He trotted toward us.

He did not make eye contact with me. Grabbing Wynn's hand, he pumped it several times.

"Have you looked around?" Yoshi asked.

"No, no—I just got here and I was telling Mike, this is all wondrous. Enormous."

"He was," I said. Yoshi still did not look at me.

"I particularly love that line over there," Wynn said. He pointed to the ditch. "What is it?" I worked to keep my face neutral as I turned, with Yoshi, to look.

We were silent for a moment.

"I planted the ditch with bamboo," Yoshi said. "Then trimmed it, so then is only suggestion of a greater height—a hedge that is not there." He grinned then, at Wynn.

"Brilliant," Wynn murmured. "Very interesting."

"There is more," Yoshi intoned.

Wynn turned to the driver, gave him instruction regarding the luggage and the car, and then put his hands together. "Michael," he said, "we'll talk later. I want Mr. Higashide to show me the grounds."

I was gracious, or at least I hoped I seemed that way. I tried to give a grin, and strolled back to the landscape building. The crew was very quiet as I barged through the open area, into my office, and slammed the door.

After I sprayed weed killer in random bursts through the courtyard, Yoshi told Wynn death was an essential part of any diorama involving life. Something about a duality. When I piled three pounds of deer droppings at the foot of the Venus, Yoshi pretended to concede to Wynn's prying, and said he had vandalized the piece to challenge himself. Each morning, the Jesus Boys continued their deliberations over the fig tree, finally deciding that a curse is God's prerogative and that any of his incarnations has the authority to divine good or evil and, making such a call, has the capacity for a curse—since from God it is not a curse, but an expression of His will. It sounded like semantics to me, like everything that spewed from Yoshi's mouth.

I spray painted an old lilac with red Rustoleum. Yoshi told Wynn the color was to highlight the essential falseness of cultivated space. Wynn loved it, and Alice said she had overheard Wynn talking about it on the phone. I uprooted one of the Katsura trees and dumped it in the driveway, and Wynn actually approached Yoshi that time and told him he thought the move interesting, but to be sure cars could still get by.

At no point did Yoshi address me. For all of the time after Wynn arrived, he acted as though I had ceased to exist. Surely, he knew I was behind the vandalism. He might have thought the first one or two things had been kids, but it had to be obvious by now that it was me, and he took credit for everything, and only after the Katsura incident did I understand why. I had been completely emasculated. Anything that happened would go back to him, good or bad. Anything could occur, and he would get credit. Moreover, Wynn would think it genius. I was staying up nights, losing sleep, risking capture and termination of my employment, all while failing to notice that my wife was more a ghost than an actual being, and it was getting me nowhere. Yoshi had removed my ability to act. He had committed a heinous act of disregard.

I stopped going out for a few nights, but then I noticed the hash marks on the condom Post-It starting to get out of hand. Wynn had not yet said anything, but if I was to be above reproach should anything happen, I had to act. On the night I did, it followed one of the last conversations I had with Jocelyn. On the phone, teary and grim, her story was classic, painful, and clear. Her sentences ended with *too much, not enough, never together.* She was elsewhere, a place I cannot now remember, but she may well have been on the other side of the world. Her voice was heavy with all I had never known about her, never cared to see, wavering as she undoubtedly spoke as much to inform me as to assert that she was somewhere, breathing, alive, beyond my reach.

Afterward, I took to the fields, this time merciless with the light. I kept it on the whole time. I heard furtive scurries, a yelp or two, enough to know I had chased off some people, and had done so without sneaking up to them and catching them in the act. I could imagine how they felt, their chests filled with the force of their own hearts, fear running through them in ways that feel so powerful, but will pale next to what they will one day come to know. Adrenaline at that age vaulted me to speeds and heights I came to desire. But a decade later, after Jocelyn was attacked, after the failure of my business, and now after Yoshi and a part of my life fading away before mauling me from beyond, after adrenaline left me unsure of my own breath, quivering with incapacity and inchoate movement, I knew to fear the rush. I heard the church kids run, imagined their arms overflowing with their clothes, the bare feet not feeling the cut and pull of forest or meadow floor, and wanted to yell to them, *you have no idea.*

As fall drew near, Alice stayed after work one night, long after the crew had gone, after Yoshi had disappeared. We drank beers on my porch, and she pressed the chilled bottle into her thigh, leaving wet circles on her pants. She told me about her father and his penchant for manicures and spa treatments, and I told her about Jocelyn and her missing arm. She picked at the paper label on her bottle while I told Jocelyn's story, and later, after a twitchy embrace, she stepped to her Audi, arms crossed against the first real chill of evening we had felt.

People experience moments when they feel nothing could get worse. You alienate a woman, fail at a job, are alone, are afraid of how small your place in the world has become. Most people recognize such assumptions later as maudlin and overwrought, usually after things *have* become worse. A select few recognize their own dramatics. Jocelyn criticized me, accurately, as too precious with myself, too wrapped up in constant acts of self-interpretation. Maybe. But whatever hit me that night trumped whatever self-control I may have possessed. It might have been the beer, might have been the odd possessions of Jocelyn's left like barbs in unexpected corners and cabinets in our house, might have been the already abstract memory of Alice's warmth against me, might have been that Yoshi had made me utterly useless, and thus emboldened. I should have seen it wouldn't be good.

Before the sun had gone down, before I was certain Yoshi was out for the night, I strode to the beech tree nearest the drive, carrying a chainsaw. I assessed the limbs, how the winds had caused the tree to grow thicker on the side toward the drive. I knew how it would fall, and as I kneeled to take the first wedge out of the tree's trunk, the rush in my ears made me envision blood. I leaned in to finish the wedge, making a deep undercut to keep the bark from pulling away at the tree's side. If Yoshi was to do this, it had to make that kind of sense. As I cut into the other side, the limbs shivered above me, then the wood split and cracked like gunfire as I stepped back. The saw died, the dark granulated with the last of the sun, and the tree shifted on its stump before crashing to the drive. The limbs shuddered, many breaking, before all was still.

At the ground, the stump's white wood shone like a moon.

With summer here, I see the Jesus Boys everyday. Though they bicker and brag, I have admitted to a few customers that I have learned from them simply by listening—debates about translators, the difference between ecumenical and evangelical readings, about the Targums and Hebrew bible, and more. I have learned much about interpretation in the last year or so, including the interpretation of one's circumstances. Now that I work at the Super-Wawa, and have become one of the three managers, the slight mental demands of the job allow me time to think.

When I work nights, when Wawa is silent with people who want to buy cigarettes and coffee but not to talk, I sometimes write to Jocelyn. I have mailed none of the letters, but I have written them anyway. At first, I tried to put into words what had happened. I tried to describe how Wynn looked at me, as if I had taken something dear to him. I defended, in writing, the action I was unable to defend the next morning, when Wynn and

Yoshi confronted me. I tried to describe Yoshi, and wrote much about how incompetent he was, but with each effort suspected my own disingenuousness. At the end of the day, Yoshi was still there. The farm still ran. I saw the crew guys from time to time, still tan, still clearly working, most ignoring me while trying to look as though they were not.

I wrote that Wynn decided to tell himself I had lost it. I tried to describe the slight and awful tremor to his hand as he gave me a card for a therapist on the day I left what had been our house. I tried, and have so far failed, to put into words what leaving that place has meant.

Once, on one of the coldest nights of the winter, I returned to the meadow, through the swale near a stream running between the perimeter fence and the church camp. I trudged through snow with only moonlight to reveal undisturbed patches of bank where I could step. I wanted to see the place again. I wanted to know everything had not been undone.

As the swale climbed up into a broad flat hilltop, I saw below into the meadow, its single beech, and beyond, to the lawn at the house. No leaves blocked the view, and the few trunks were all shadow and suggestion. The Katsura grove still stood, a tight smudge of night in the midst of the drifting expanse of white. I could see the main house, and around it what appeared to be headstones. After a long wait, I strode into the meadow to see what Yoshi had put there. Several steps later, I could see. They were bronze and hammered, catching what little light met them. Ovate, toothed, deeply ribbed, standing against the snow as something between memorial and a sign of warding, they were sculptures. Sculpted beech leaves.

PRAYER

Each week the CDs arrive, four shows on two discs, in a padded envelope, the same loopy secretary script of her address. Inside is not the voice of God so much as a voice about God, and she is to type everything said, so that the penitent but hard-of-hearing can turn on closed captioning. Jesus when written has not nearly the weight of texture as when the show's host uses it—as a bludgeon, as a sly suggestion, as a four-syllable paroxysm of joy: Ja-HEE-zuss-AH! She used to be tempted to write it that way, just once, to try and slip it in, to see if viewers would notice or care, if they, too, were caught up in the passion of testimony.

But that was before Nelson disappeared. Before the winter when his residency gave him night sweats, before he would awaken with a start, sometimes a scream. Before she would find him some nights standing naked in the light of the refrigerator, the hair covering him blue from the light there, and she would take his hand and lead him to bed. Before she started waking herself, to touch where he should be, to make sure he was near and had not wandered off. Before she woke one night to a crystalline snow and wind so harsh it turned the windblown snow to a glassy fog, a night when she slid her arm across to find the sheets cold, doors ajar, and a path of fading footsteps in a line to the woods.

They found him slumped against a tree almost a mile from the house, his eyes closed and encased in ice, his hair tufted with snow.

Now, some nights she finds sense in the preacher's words. When he talks of the wounds of the Savior, she thinks of Nelson's feet, whether they were cut in the woods, how he never felt the cold all around him. Or if he did, what he thought it was, on what vision he floated, what blessing he sought, what voices guided him. She knows when she thinks of him it is a form of prayer and that on the coldest nights, when she walks bare-legged as far as she can, until the pain of the cold drives her back to the house, she is offering her flesh to bring back his. She wants to say to the woods, *Take this, my flesh and blood. Eat. Drink. Do this in memory of him.*

LAST WORDS

I.

First sunlight and still the family is there. All night they have sat, watching the dull rise of Edward's chest with grim relief, then waiting as it withers under the wrinkle of yellowing sheets, as they feel in their own chests a sympathetic tightening, as if their breathing were restricted by his reluctant lungs. Each time he inhales anew, a wave moves through the room, and even the candle Marta has lit wobbles with the cycle's renewal. Gareth, Edward's son, sees how pretty Marta is even in devastation, even with her eyes rimmed and her cheeks drawn into the frown her mouth has become in the last week.

Gareth thinks that she should not be as close to this man as she seems to have become, and he wonders if there is something in her past he does not yet know that compels her to find more sorrow in the prolonged passing of this man who is not yet even her father-in-law, and who it now appears never will be. Beside her, Misako, Edward's third wife and the most recent person Edward has insisted upon Gareth referring to as a mother, is as unyielding as her husband's chest. Each woman appears unaware or unconcerned of the other's presence, and Gareth is surprised at how reluctant he is to say anything to either one.

Within the folds of the sheets, the shadows shorten. The room's particulars grow into definition—the antique map of the Great Lakes, mounted in an oak frame over the head of the cherry sleigh bed; the hardbound books—the artwork of Klee, Miro, de Kooning, and Pollock; books on Ennio Morricone, the Tbilisi Avant-garde, and Peter Blake; manuals on Shaker furniture, machinists, stonemasonry, and more—all stacked and topped with a sheet of glass to form a sideboard across from the foot of the bed; the carved Moroccan screen cordoning off the master bath; the layered Kazakh rugs patchworking the floor; the chocolaty leather club chairs that the three vigilants have pulled to the bedside; the austere photographs of his buildings, framed in birch and other blond woods, hung across from the window and beginning to reflect the increasing light in the room. What was to have been a warm room, to have been a sanctuary, now feels to Gareth as a fitting tomb.

Marta says, "Breakfast. I can make breakfast if anyone wants anything."

Gareth almost expresses his surprise; she has never cooked for him, or for anyone, as far as he knows. Instead, he says, "We can have Timothy run out for something."

Timothy has the misfortune of being Edward's last intern, arriving to have his mentor suffer two heart attacks and a stroke, all within two weeks, late in the young man's semester. In the week since Edward had been confined to his bedroom, Timothy's internship has consisted of running errands for the family, turning away well-intentioned but inappropriate visitors, and beginning to anticipate his role in helping with organizing the estate, the papers, and more. Gareth has contacted the boy's family and the college, has expressed his willingness to release the young man from the obligations, to evaluate him for time spent and to provide references, and both the college and the intern's parents have left the decision to Timothy to gauge, to figure out his usefulness.

In the few conversations Gareth has had with him, Timothy has expressed his sense of duty to "the man he admires" and has assured Gareth that he is learning a great deal, and feels that as long as he can learn and be of service at a difficult time, he'll stick around. Gareth admires the boy's sense of duty and dedication, as well as his intelligence. While the tasks he has performed have been generally menial, he has shown a character and perspicacity that Gareth knows everyone has appreciated having present and willing to assist.

"Bagels, coffee, some fruit, the usual?" Gareth asks the women. Marta nods and Misako has no reaction.

"I'll get Tim," he says. As Gareth stands, his father begins a noisy inhale again as a pair of blue jays bash and rustle against the window. No one, he realizes, is filling Edward's feeders. Hopefully, Tim will know where to find birdseed in Queens.

He leaves his father's room and sees the door to the study ajar. He assumes Tim has arisen, and so steps in to get a pen and paper to make a list. As he does, he sees the boy is still asleep, on the foldout couch, the blankets having washed off of him in the night. He is sprawled and nearly naked but for a pair of briefs, and his skin is so pale as to be nearly blue. But it is without blemish or other mark, and the line running from his neck to his navel is a lightly shadowed groove. Gareth is struck by the beauty of this man, at the surprising spectacle of his body, and has the urge to cover him. Instead, he retrieves a pen from the desk near the door, and a blank index card, and leaves.

In the hall, he hears his father rasp, "Nothing was as great as him!" The force stops Gareth in the hall for a moment, and a chill rips over his chest. By the time Gareth steps into the room, Edward Rawlings is dead, and Misako, who had sat for a week unmoved, is now sobbing and beating the dead man's chest while Marta weeps into her hands.

II.

Timothy starts at the sound of someone shouting his name. He realizes it is Gareth, and that the raw note he has not heard is there because Edward must have died. Edward is dead. He feels as though he might vomit, and so stands and scans the room for the wastebasket, a potted plant, anything that will suffice, but in standing the feeling leaves him. Pulling on rumpled chinos, he tries to breathe deeply, to still the terror and sorrow rising in him, to stop thinking about the feel of the man, of his shoulders, how his arm would reach up to encircle his waist, how his fingers would stroke the small of his back, the surprise he had first felt in the delight of Edward, and how he had fought the memories during the reality that the past week had afforded him.

Pulling on his t-shirt, he hears Marta saying, between sobs, "What do you think it means? Why would he say that?"

"It's not some conversion, if that's what you think," Gareth says. Timothy wonders if Gareth has any idea how condescending he sounds when he speaks to Marta. How Gareth would react if he knew some of the things Edward had observed about his son, the disappointment that would slow his steps as he spoke with Tim, their walks suddenly slowed as he lamented. How Edward had felt sympathy for Marta, how he had shared that with Tim, someone Gareth would no doubt consider the lowly intern. So many things Gareth didn't know about the intern. "Just write it down, for now," Gareth says. "We can figure it out later." Then, he shouts again, "Tim!"

Timothy bounds across the hall. "What? What? Has he . . . passed?"

Gareth nods once. Misako starts to wail again.

Marta appears at his side, pulling at his hand. "He said something, he was out of it, not conscious, and then he just sits up and says, 'Nothing is so great as him!'"

Gareth says, "That's not what he said."

"Well it was like that—" she looks at Timothy. "What could he have meant?"

Timothy looked at her and then at Gareth. "Who knows? Really, it could have been anything. I don't feel like I know him well enough, you know, to tell."

III.

Evan will never forget the morning he saw two women having breakfast in bed in the architect's apartment. He had seen it all from the porch off his kitchen, suspended far above the build-

ing's courtyard—designed and planted by Edward, of course—
near the corner where his wing of the building joined Edward's.
The women read the paper, while Edward sat a ways away in
a chair. He wore only a pair of loose and holey pants, and the
women wore tank tops, white. Their arms, milky and pale, rested against one another, their shoulders meeting, their entire
posture that of lovers, and their gaze, when it drifted to Edward,
was both frankly bawdy and coy. The curtains were sheer and
white, the rumpled bed was white, the dishes on which they ate
were white—the entire scene was white. He stood on the porch,
long having stopped the pretense of watering impatiens, locked
on the sight, until Edward stood and kissed one of the women,
and then the other. When Evan fled inside his apartment then,
the scene was all he could think about for weeks. Though he
never saw either of them again, they lived within him, appearing in dreams or surprising him in idle moments with the force
of recollection.

Years later, he sits in his apartment, considering whether or
not to paint it, when he hears through the open window, *Nothing else created him!* He realizes the voice is Edward's, but it
sounded too feeble, too much like a wheeze, and then it occurs
to him that it had to have been Edward, and then he knew the
worst: the building had buzzed with the sudden decline in their
licentious neighbor, and now Evan realizes he may have heard
the last thing Edward Rawlings would ever say.

For the next week, each morning he heads to the mailboxes,
breaks into Edward's by gouging the floor of his own up and out,
and takes his neighbor's mail. Each time he does, he carries it
back to his apartment and lights each piece on fire and lets it
flare and smolder in his fire grate. He burns it each day, until

Sunday, when there is no mail, and the break makes him stop.

Edward's shout was thrust out of him as if it were a prayer, a last cast toward faith from a man whose throat knew neither supplication nor benediction. A thick throat in a proud neck. He wore shirts with collars so soft that they almost draped his neck, curled into his shoulders, so soft it took a tie to hold them up, a tie with a florid knot large and silken as a woman's fist. The softness of his skin and the pride in his throat and the ornament of his dress combined as an affront to God. Perhaps in his last moments he atoned and called out a truth he had discovered.

Evan believes in God, knows what it feels to be quickened with the knowledge of a creator—though the word *creator* is a failure of language. The word he seeks is between creator, seer, presence, and palpability, all of those things—the best combination he has for when, more than three decades ago, in the weeks after his wife had gone (bad brakes, river, hand pounding ever more weakly at a stubborn window crowded with greasy bubbles), he had helped his daughter again to get ready for school on one of the blurred days that made January warm with loss. Pulling her hair back, he saw the red swell of her right earlobe, an earring like a silver sliver of rage, and when he pulled it out and she winced, pus oozed onto his finger, followed by blood, her cries, and a chill that shot the length of his spine until his chest burned. He had not noticed, had no idea how far the infection went, did not know what to tell her to stop her crying.

It was not a miracle that he found it. It was not that he believed some god showed him the presence of the wound. It was that he realized in that moment the vastness of chance, of a universe that held together despite its tendency to want to fall apart, and that the hold had to be a matter of some divine will.

And the will came first, came before anything else came to be, before anything else was created.

Nothing else created him. An easy exhortation, an easy realization, it turned out, when confronted with all you are not and can never be.

IV.

The army taught Nolan how to walk. More than just the position of his shoulders, the use of the balls of his feet, more than keeping his torso aligned with his hips—they taught him that the first best thing was to move. To keep moving. To do and to get done. As he opened the gate on the morning of Edward's death, he heard the man himself shout to him, in a frothy bark, "Nolan cut the Acer's limb."

So he walked. His employer had the force of an officer, even now, even while dying. The man knew he was dying and, early in the week, had given his gardener short litanies of instructions. *The Pyrus must be trimmed. Nolan, the astilbe corms, remember. Nolan, divide the hemerocallis, the hosta, the convallaria. Bring the pyracantha under control.* And some of his instructions were simply cautions to monitor the state of plants—*Nolan, the Acer. Nolan, the Katsura. Nolan, the Cotinus.*

At the sound of the morning's order, Nolan heard the effort and the sadness and, perhaps, even the desperation that this possibly last order be carried out. He froze on the walk, waiting to hear more, feeling that he should go to the man. After a moment, he cursed his indecision lightly under his breath, pulled the gate closed behind him, and strode to the back garden.

The chainsaw started with one pull. Its engine rang off the brick surrounding him on three sides, the sound jangling despite the Edenic surroundings. No number of leaves or fronds could mask the cutting sound, and when he lowered the whirring blade to the gray flesh of the tree's errant limb, the limb Edward discussed several times over the years, the limb he questioned whether it should be left to grow to see if it *would* add to the garden or whether it would mar in ways not yet known, the limb that tested the limits of the man's control. The bark's gray shredded to white and a torrent of dust shot onto Nolan's legs, his shoes, the ground around him, like snow. Then the limb lurched, the chain of the saw caught, and the blade kicked out, back up toward Nolan's face.

It moved as slowly as anything he had ever witnessed. It gave him enough time to turn, to dive to the side, but not enough time to move completely. He saw it bite into his thigh before he felt it. But once he felt the bite, the chain's pull on the muscle, his pants twist as if to wring the blood from his leg, he collapsed and the saw died as it hit a rock, and he only heard a scream he could not believe was his own.

V.

The hallway is twice as long, three times as long, incomprehensibly longer than it has ever been. And loud. Each step a desperate thrust of bone on wood. Tim wants to be quiet, yearns for cover, for seconds and other sounds, but in the apartment now frozen with sorrow, it is as if all sound and texture have been peeled away. No mercy for those with tasks yet to do.

His shirt is a chore to button. His shoes, though they slip on, loathe him. Delay him. He considers where to go, where to get the bagels, the breakfast, the seed—and what is nearby. His hope is for fire, for water, something consuming. Edward's journals were leather, filled with excellent paper, *paper that can take ink*, he always said. He was the only man Tim ever knew—and perhaps the last man in Queens—still to insist on a fountain pen. It was a minor annoyance now transformed to a difficulty for Tim.

No one gets the pages, Tim! Let Gareth and that submissive shrew, that sham of a wife, try to figure out what Edward said. It is clear as day to Tim. The man's last wish is for Tim to destroy the journals he has kept.

The subway rattles and bumps, the corners of the journals stabbing at his ribs, their insistence at his skin something like penance. He is not the only one aware of the train's rocky procedure, how it is worse today. Faces around him register the difficulty, legs tense, hands float ready for the next jolt. Across from where he sits, a woman in black looks at her lap. Her shoulders shake and spasm with what he realizes are not movements to steady herself but are tears. As she lifts an earring to place it in her lobe, the train rocks and the stone flashes as it drops neatly into the cleft between her breasts. She scans the floor; her crying starts to climb in intensity. He wants to lean, to tell her, but then he hears her sobs, sees the shake in her jaw, and then Edward's breath is with him, Edward's eyes and hands are in the bag, his voice is the rattle of steel and the careening of the car. The woman's face is contorted now.

In Newark there are fires. Fires burn on the Lower East Side. But he has no idea where to find fire in Queens. But there will be fire somewhere, smoldering, anonymous, a world away from where his Edward has died. And he away from that world now, knows what Edward would do, for whatever reason. He kneels, then, steadies himself against the rock, and takes her waving hand. "It's OK," he says. "I have to tell you where the earring is. I happened to see it drop."

She appears to scarcely understand. But when she sniffles, it is clear she waits. "It dropped," he says, nodding toward her chest. "It's in your shirt." She smiles, and then she laughs once, and turns from him to retrieve it. In her hand, a veil, a small hat. She places it on the seat, and once the earring is in her ear, she calms. The train rattles like a chainsaw, and he wonders then about Nolan, the last roar he heard in the yard, and some father yelling in the neighborhood.

What small things mean comfort. A block off the Boulevard, a vacant lot, low smolder of a barrel fire. He stokes it, feeds it paper like communion.

VI.

It was easily forty years since Gareth had thought of Kim in any way other than passing, or in explanation to others of how his parents—his father, his aloof, activist and pickled mother, the succession of waifs who followed after her death—could maintain their schedules and projects and appearances and still raise a child. The answer, Gareth enjoyed saying wryly, or with feigned depth and injury, as if knowing the enormity of perceived abandonment, was that *they* did not *raise* him. Kim did. Mostly Kim. There were others—a driver, Edward's assistants, young men from Bard or Vassar or Columbia—but mostly Kim.

Kim had studied German and art history at New Rochelle, and mastered both sufficiently to impress Edward in conversation. Or so he said publicly. Broad of face and hips, bony and long-limbed, Edward was fond of saying she was clearly from working stock, and would admit, privately, that those characteristics were what actually drew him to her. Her very presence suggested a work ethic rooted in generational memory. Everything about her was clear—her skin, her eyes, her gaze, the translucent brown of her hair, the simple solid colors of her clothes, most of which were handmade but with such care and precision that most people assumed they were tailored by someone with exceptionally plain taste. *She's practically Mennonite*, Edward said.

Gareth was barely into his teens when he realized what had to be going on, why he would come upon them standing in the stairwell indecisive about what to do with their hands and their chins, or why she came along on their trips to the house in Branford, or why she would appear in the study or the kitchen flushed and distracted. The way she dealt with him became more wistful as he grew older. Sometimes her knuckly hand would rest on the back of his neck a moment too long, or she would push hair from his face while he watched the dodgy black-and-white television Edward tolerated in a back room. He caught her watching him.

She ultimately oversaw the death of Gareth's mother, bringing her water, warm cloths, later sneaking her valium, painkillers, quarterlies, chocolate. In his memory of the final months of his mother's life, Kim was forever adjusting the blinds to keep what little granular light the building's angles allowed from getting in her charge's glassy eyes. Edward kept out of the room, kept busy, kept to drawings and meetings and smoking where he thought she could not smell it. Edward kept his eye on the years to come, on the accommodating waist and thighs of his wife's and son's caretaker.

And now, this, his last, deranged, sweat-stained outburst, revealing the letch at the heart of things, the man he always knew his father was, the man he himself struggled never to become, his last words: *No one was a lay like Kim.*

VII.

Noble are the seraphim. His vanity is such that he chooses to use the word seraphim, to decorate some kind of deathbed conversion, some kind of final appeal to the God he so forcefully scorned to her. *I am not surprised*, Misako insists to herself. She says it repeatedly in her head. She very much wants not to be surprised.

She knows he was venal, brash, cruel. In the moment of his death, she keeps her head still, but mentally reviews the contents of the room. The map—how inaccurate it was, how silly to have a map made by people who had no idea what they drew. The bed, a horizontal throne he hardly ever slept in, an insomniac wanderer. And when not wandering out of sleeplessness, wandering as a wolf, an unreconstructed philanderer—which made her, well, she wasn't sure. The ridiculous books made into a table. Knowledge is not an ornament, yet he wore it that way constantly. He only read books—and the strangest ones he could muster—so that he could say unexpected things to others and could count on usually being the uncontested authority of his strange subjects in whatever room he ended up holding forth.

Yet he could speak to you, find your mouth in a room, in a car, in a park even, in such a way that to converse with him was to kiss him. Or so she always thought. Contrasted to all of her own family's distance, the thrill of Edward came from proximity. Even on the phone, a conversation with Edward involved her skin, her fingers, his breath.

And now this utterance, this talk of angels, a man so corporeal suddenly pining for the ineffable. He who would boast that Japanese minimalism—*her* passion, though not as neatly reduced as he loved to make it, with his terminology—*her* minimalism was simply a fear of the chaos contained in the real world. He who disdained faith in others, who resented his own long-lapsed Catholicism, despite retaining the penchant for cursing and the love of ceremony.

He mocked her faith, though it only resulted in making her more quiet about it. How many times had she sat at the cramped table in the kitchen and said the Rosary under her breath while he loitered in his study or traveled? How many times had she lit a candle for him on impulse passing St. Peter's or St. Mark's? How many times had his name and her list of minor betrayals composed the oration in the confessional, and how many times had she thought of *this* day, of what it will take to have a mass said for him?

She considers what he has said, how it might be enough to mention to Father Wojtowicz, how it might be what it will take to have the mass said. How his last words, though wrong, silly, even perhaps a lie, might be the very thing to save him.

She turns from the body, to the sound of Timothy scurrying about, panicked, his furtiveness all but gone. Nolan is shouting somewhere. And her husband, now dead, decided his dying words should be some sham of Christianity. How very far she is from home. How very far she has come from anything of her own.

VIII.

Marta can barely remember Finland. It is the fanciful setting of her grandfather's stories—she hardly thinks of the stories as his life, given the distance of the place. But she was once a girl there, she has long been told, and once the sort of child who did everything she should have. Her grandfather used to say she had been born properly—a short labor, an easy push (comparatively), a full wail and spirited latch to her mother's breast—and so her agreeable manner and quiet disposition meant she strode well over the earth. His words.

He himself had known how to walk, a notion she had only thought of recently, having talked to Edward's gardener a bit about it. In the town of her birth, her grandfather had been a well-respected obstetrician prior to her family having to move to America. She knew and had heard repeated by her mother tales of him snowshoeing across drifts to arrive at the delivery room from their tidy home nearby.

And once in the states, her father having carried on in *his* father's profession, she recalls the stories from her childhood from when they lived near Rochester, in a speck of a town frequently lashed with snow, how he had endured the harsh winters and the crushing work of the postwar rush of children being born to returning GIs. Their home was, at the right time of day and in the right season, literally in the shadow of the hospital. Built atop a hill above town in the years when healthcare meant fresh air, even by the forties it still had its long porches and striped canvas awnings over the tall windows.

The solariums threw sunlight back over the brick details. The most famous picture of her father's career, and the enduring image she has of him, long after his passing, in a room not unlike Edward's, was of him standing in a nursery so crowded that bassinets were perched on straight-back chairs, overturned washtubs, and chipped end tables, because they had ran out of the usual carts. Her father had delivered 7 babies to 5 mothers in 9 hours, a tale that was told again and again in all the towns back to the Great Lakes, the same evening the first snow of the new year buried the town in more than two feet of snow. Two of the mothers were brought to the hospital on the hill pulled on sleds by workhorses unaccustomed to the climb or the temperature. One of the horses froze to death outside the hospital, its owner asleep inside, having succumbed to the whiskey he drank on the ride over to keep warm.

Her father would snowshoe from the hospital during the blizzards that buffeted the country that year. She would help her mother bring tea pots to the upper bedroom of their house, where she would hand the pot to him through a second story window, dainty china pot wrapped in one of his wool shirts, the leaves in a basket tucked in the folds, and he would tramp back across the snow dunes, holding the blob of wool aloft like one of the gifts of the magi. Her father, walking on frozen water, hot over cold, life battling death, rise and fall of sleeping mothers and infants and invalids and the slowly dying.

And her father, for all of his heroism and the large shadow his life cast over the community, would beat her mother. It seldom occurred, and was never spoken of, and she never witnessed it personally. But she felt it long before her mother told her of it, and in the years when she knew, she knew rage, but little of what to do.

And she thought of him now, looking at a dead man who would have been something of a father to her. He had blathered something. At first, she believed he had said, *No one is too late for heaven*, but she dismissed it as a feverish slur, the vocal equivalent of a hallucination. Whatever he said, she knew, was not the truth. Like her own father, there was more. There were many people in that body—at least one for every person in that room standing vigil. Her own would-be husband, for instance—

Essentially six or seven people have died today, she thinks. It was unclear which, if any of them, were the true holders of that life. Her father's stories, her grandfather's mythology, Edward's stories—the world was scarcely believable the way men told of it.

ACKNOWLEDGMENTS

The stories in this collection originally appeared, in slightly different forms, in the following journals:

Cream City Review: Communion
Georgia Review: Nguyen Van Thieu is Dead at 78
Iron Horse Literary Review: The Mechanics of Heat
Mid-American Review: The Visions of Edwin Miller
New Letters: Beautiful for a Day, A Country of Shoes, Last Words
PANK: Pick Up, Unemployed
Quarter After Eight: Bourbon and Milk, Prayer
Southern Review: Groundscratchers
Tupelo Quarterly: Twins

Enormous thanks to the folks at Tolsun Books for their enthusiasm for this collection and the care they have taken with it. Thank you to Risa Pappas and Kalani Pickhart for their careful reading and helpful suggestions on the stories. Thanks also to Heather Lang-Cassera, David and Brandi Pischke, and Margarita Cruz for their support and assistance with the logistics of shepherding a manuscript into a book.

I am grateful to the trusted friends who read these stories and offered helpful critiques, chiefly and most especially to J. David Stevens. To the editors who chose to publish the stories—Mike Czyzniejewski, T.R. Hummer, Robert Stewart, M. Bartley Siegel and Roxane Gay, Cara Blue Adams, Chris Fink, Leslie Jill Patterson, Brad Aaron Modlin, Christina Veladota and Thom Conroy, and Jessamyn Smith—my deep thanks for your past support of my writing and, more broadly, for the work you do.

Several of the stories owe a debt to people met during the decade and a half I spent in the landscaping and horticulture industries. To the grunts, landscrapers, mulch loaders, growers, nurserymen, designers, florists, and people who started with just a lawnmower, pick-up truck and drive (much love to the late Al Petrin), those years and friendships meant more to me than you can ever know. And to my brother, Dave, who was there with me for most of it, I hope you get a kick out of some of these stories.

I earned my MFA in fiction at Penn State and am grateful for what I learned from my professors there: Charlotte Holmes, Bill Cobb, and the late Peter Schneeman, whose careful line editing has made me very fussy indeed when revising.

Finally, thank you to my family, Jill, Bella and Annie. I am very aware that their affection and support have made writing possible for me, and that many others do not enjoy such a privilege.

To my parents, to whom this book is dedicated, thank you for the lore you helped me access, the interesting places we lived, and the curiosity you cultivated that led to this. And to my mom, Camille, I am ever thankful for the anecdote that led to the title story of this book.

For nearly 15 years, **Gabriel Welsch** worked in the ornamental horticulture and landscaping industries in roles as a crew grunt, production grower, plant buyer, landscape foreman, and garden designer before working in higher education teaching and administration. He writes fiction and poetry, and is the author of four collections of poems: *The Four Horsepersons of a Disappointing Apocalypse, The Death of Flying Things, An Eye Fluent in Gray,* and *Dirt and All Its Dense Labor.* His work has appeared widely, in journals including *Mid-American Review, Ploughshares, Georgia Review, New Letters, Southern Review, Chautauqua, Harvard Review, Ascent,* and on *Verse Daily* and in Ted Kooser's column "American Life in Poetry." A native of Maine and a graduate of the MFA program at Penn State, he now lives in Pittsburgh, Pennsylvania, with his family, and works as vice president of marketing and communications at Duquesne University.

CPSIA information can be obtained
at www.ICGtesting.com
Printed in the USA
FSHW021229290721
83519FS